Follow
the
Moon

Herm Rawlings

ISBN: 9798648895775

Cover design by Dawn Spears.

https://scanticbooks.blogspot.com
Facebook: Scantic Books

Dedication

The two biggest influences in my life have been there from the start. In fact, if it weren't for them, I wouldn't be here at all. The past few years have been extremely challenging for them, and my love and admiration has done nothing but continue to grow. Thank you for all you have done for me. For teaching me right from wrong, always providing what I needed (not necessarily what I wanted ... lol), and allowing me to learn by making mistakes. And when I did screw up, teaching me to accept the consequences no matter how small or how harsh. Because of you, I am the man, the husband. and the father I am today. As you were always there for me, I will now be there for you.

Mom and Dad, this is for you.

Chapter One

The waters were calm as the sun rose on the tiny coastal town of Chincoteague Island, Virginia. The locals pronounced the island's name "shink-ah-teeg" and could always identify a tourist by the way they struggled with the name.

This was a beautiful early June day for the four friends who had just navigated their boat from Curtis Merritt Harbor, the largest of the few public boat ramps located on the small Eastern Shore island. Their grand plan was to have a relaxing day of fishing and then head to shore and enjoy some drinks at Chatties Lounge, a popular local watering hole, before heading back to the rental house for a good night's sleep and heading out on the water again in the morning.

The four friends had a hard time arranging get-togethers these days because they each had jobs and lived in various parts of the country. But, after much scheduling and rescheduling, they all managed to get time off on the same dates and get back together after a two-year break. The longtime friends had no idea when they would see each other again, so they vowed that this extended weekend would be their best one yet.

Richard Drewer guided the 2001, thirty-foot, Grady-White Marlin slowly through the waters of the Chincoteague Channel and gradually inched the throttle up as the boat approached the inlet flowing into the open sea. When he reached the ocean side of the inlet, he pushed the throttle forward to full power and headed east.

After cruising for about an hour, the boat arrived at Blackfish Banks, an artificial reef 5.8 nautical miles southeast of Assateague Beach. The reef had been established in phases as part of "Operation Reef-Ex '98" when forty armored personnel carriers and tanks from the Army National Guard were sunk and scattered in the area sixty to seventy feet below the surface. A second phase in 2003 added fifty New York City MTA "Redbird" subway cars to the site, and even more subway cars were added in June and December of 2008.

The reef was always a good spot to catch structure-oriented fish such as Sea Bass but was also usually good for Flounder and Trout and, if they were lucky, they could reel in an Amberjack, Jack Crevalle, or possibly a shark or two that might be cruising the area.

Richard pulled back the throttle control of the twin Yamaha V250 horsepower outboard engines and slowed the boat as it approached a large yellow buoy with "8A" in bold letters on the top. He kidded that this must be the place as he pointed towards the words "Blackfish Banks Artificial Reef" that were printed in large black letters on it.

"Hey Traise," Richard yelled, "head up to the bow and get ready to drop the anchor."

Traise Robbins stared at him with a *who me?* look. "What the hell do I know about dropping an anchor?"

Richard stared back at him feigning disgust. "Really? Didn't you work at Capt. Bob's Marina one summer when we were in school? Get your ass up on the bow, pick up the anchor if it's not too heavy for you, and drop it overboard when I say so. And for God's sake, stay clear of the chain or Katie will be spending all that life insurance money on things that you wouldn't buy for her."

The two men were life-long friends who grew up together on Chincoteague Island. After high school, Richard enlisted in the Coast Guard, and Traise went on to college at James Madison University in Harrisonburg, Virginia. Since graduating with a Bachelor in Media Arts and Design, he had ascended the corporate ladder and was now a department supervisor at an up-and-coming media company in northern Virginia. Always in touch with one another, the two men were more like brothers than friends even now in their mid-thirties. Each was the other's best man in their weddings, and, although they didn't see each other that much anymore, when they did get together, it was as if nothing had changed.

Traise looked at the other two men on the boat. "Knew I should have ordered those t-shirts," he joked as he headed to the bow.

"What t-shirts?" asked Richard.

"The ones that say, 'Our Captain is a Dick!'" Traise shot back.

"Better a dick than a ginger," Richard responded, referring to his buddy's red, curly hair.

Johnny Gendo chuckled at the constant ripping between Richard and Traise. "Guess it's beer from now on," he said to no one in particular as he took the last sip of his caramel café latte and placed the cup in the plastic bag that was brought with them for trash. "Need anything Sam?" Johnny asked.

Sam Willow looked up from leaning over the side of the boat where he had been for the last thirty minutes and uttered, "A new stomach and some pavement would be nice."

This was Sam's first experience on the water, not counting the log ride at Busch Gardens, and he wasn't dealing with it very well so far.

"You'll never see me anywhere closer to the water than my bathtub from now on," Johnny said and snickered at his friend as he unlatched the lid of the large blue cooler, dug in through the ice, and pulled out a Guinness Stout. "Guess next time you'll think twice before drinking half a bottle of Tequila the night before going out on a boat."

Sam pulled his head up and looked at Johnny with half-open eyes, let out a faint "Ugh," and resumed his position.

The three men were college friends, with Johnny and Traise being roommates the entire four years of college in both the dorm as well as the townhouse they rented during their junior and senior year. When they first met, Traise wasn't so sure about his new roomie, with his long hair, nerdy computer talk and all, but they quickly became best friends. After college, Johnny had always seemed to get bit by the love bug and never hesitated to pick up and move to wherever the new love of his life resided. The last episode ended with him moving to, and still living in, Spokane, Washington. Although that relationship didn't last, he was quite content with his new location. The last time he had seen the other three was when he flew in for Traise's wedding two years ago. As usual, things just picked up right where they left off.

Sam was a different story. Although he met Traise and Johnny at college, nobody could quite remember when or under what circumstances.

The popular theory was that he showed up one night to the wrong house for a party and, after mingling among the crowd for an hour or so, realized that he didn't know anybody. But with half a bottle of Tequila downed, he determined it didn't matter who these people were. They seemed nice to him, so what the hell. And with that, Sam and his always cheerful mood were in the circle and a permanent member of the "Band of Brothers." Although a bit mellower than the early days, he was still known as the King of Tequila with his ever-growing collection of unusual Tequila bottles.

During one of his many visits to see Traise in Harrisonburg, Richard had met and immediately connected with Gendo and Sam. The four fast friends remained close ever since.

When Traise got to the bow, Richard pulled back the throttle into the neutral position and, after a slow drift toward the buoy, yelled, "Okay, let her go!" Traise tossed the anchor over the front of the bow and stepped aside as the chain fed out until the anchor hit bottom at sixty feet. The boat was now in position thirty yards from the buoy, and, as long as the anchor held, they would stay in the same general position while they fished. With the anchor grabbing and the engine switched off, Richard looked at the electronic depth and fish finder and saw that the day looked promising as the readout indicated that there were quite a few fish at various depths around them.

"Let's get some lines in the water you land-lubbers!" Richard called out as he began inserting multiple fishing rods into the side-mounted holders of the boat. He then brought out the bait cooler and showed the three how to attach the strips of squid to a two-hook rig on each pole. Once all six lines were in the water and at the right depth, Richard announced, "All right boys, time to relax and see what we may get for dinner tonight."

Even though the four were always joking with one another, when it came to the boat and being out on the water, Traise, Sam, and Johnny all knew it was Richard in charge, at least out here. He had plenty of boat experience gained during his nine years in the Coast Guard as a Boatswain's Mate. Navigating the waters around the local area and even further offshore was second nature to him.

When he left the Coast Guard, Richard started his own business, traveling the states with his dog Sprig, a lovable golden lab, and "picking" vintage items from wherever he could find them and bringing them back to his small but popular store in the little coastal town of New Bern, North Carolina. After a few years to get the business firmly established, he finally earned enough to purchase the used but still in great condition fishing boat. When the details of their current trip were confirmed, he loaded the boat on the trailer and made the five-hour drive up the coast to Chincoteague to hang with the boys for the weekend. They were equals on land, but in this environment, "Captain Dick" was in charge.

"We'll hang here for a bit and see if we get anything," Richard said. "If not, we'll pull up the anchor and drift a little while and see if we can get some Flounder."

Sam seemed to be doing a little better since they stopped moving. He had re-located to one of the padded seats by the stern but still wasn't saying much as the other three grabbed beers and settled in. Richard turned on the satellite radio and tuned to the 90's station. "Just make sure you keep an eye on those lines. If you see one being pulled down, give a shout." And as he held up his beer, he gave his favorite captain's order: "Otherwise, enjoy boys. Here's a toast to us. Good to be with you again."

As they relaxed, watched their lines, and reminisced about the good old days, there was no way they could foresee that this day would end up being the longest day of their lives.

* * *

Thirty-two miles away from the four friends in their fishing boat, the Cessna 172P began to pick up speed quickly as it rolled down the 4070-foot asphalt runway designated "14/32" at the Ocean City Municipal Airport. Although the name would indicate that the small airport was located within the geographical confines of the popular Maryland beach resort, it was actually a few miles away in Berlin, Maryland, a quaint, artsy town that had found its own identity and was recently voted by a travel magazine as one of the "coolest small towns" in the country.

When he reached optimal speed for take-off, Steve Adams gently pulled back on the control yoke of the white, two-seat, single-engine plane. The nose gently angled upward into the calm and clear sky. At five hundred feet of altitude, Steve turned the plane into a slow bank to the left while still climbing until he reached a heading of 180 degrees, which established his flight direction as due south of the airport. After ascending, he finally leveled off at four-thousand feet, powered back the engine to a speed of 120 miles per hour, and, after scouring the sky around him for any other aircraft, adjusted his harness to be a bit more comfortable.

The fifty-six-year-old had taken up flying twenty years ago as a way to get away from the hustle and bustle of daily life as well as the constant stress from his job as a divorce lawyer. A year after obtaining his pilot's license, he found the 1981 Cessna for sale at the local airport and, after a short negotiation and a test flight, he agreed to purchase the aircraft. He always despised the hassle of renting a plane. Even though owning a plane was more expensive than renting, he decided that having his own wings would give him more peace of mind regarding safety, availability, maintenance, and the craft's overall air worthiness.

This was the first chance he had to get back in the air in a while because the last two months had been packed with almost constant negotiations between his latest client and her husband's attorney. Usually, his cases were fairly quick and clean, but this one was anything but. Property division, life insurances, vehicles, medical and dental costs for the children, even who got the family pets were all points of contention. Lesson learned from this case? If you are married (which he was not and had no intention of being), do not have an affair and, if you do, do not be stupid enough to have text messages and pictures of your mistress on your phone. Especially if you and your wife decided long ago to share the same password on your phones because neither had anything to hide. *Dumbass*, Steve had thought in the presence of his client more than a few times.

With the case finally concluded (and with a very nice retainer fee paid in full), Steve decided to take advantage of the predicted calm weather on this Saturday and take a nice relaxing flight to blow off some steam. He adjusted his course slightly to the east, putting him about five miles off the coast and heading south.

He enjoyed this flight area the most of any because it gave him views of two different worlds. On one side was the ocean with its large expansion of nothingness. He may see a few fishing boats, oil tankers, or cargo ships here and there but mostly just the vast expanse of the Atlantic Ocean. In the past, he was able to see the occasional whale surfacing and expelling water from its blowhole as it filled its lungs with air before diving back down to the ocean depths. On the other side were the remote beaches of the lower Eastern Shore of Maryland and Virginia. Although populated, the lower shore was one of the last undeveloped coastal areas anywhere along the Atlantic Ocean. His flight would take him along Assateague National Seashore, home of the famous wild ponies, and beyond that, Chincoteague Island, home of some of his favorite seafood restaurants. He'd have to plan a visit for some good eating in the near future.

He would fly just a little bit further south before turning around and heading back home. Not a long flight, but long enough to clear his head, listen to nothing but the constant hum of the plane's engine and take in Mother Nature in all her glory. Even though he had to constantly monitor his instruments and the surrounding sky, the freedom and calmness of feeling like being a bird in the sky without a worry always energized him. This would be a nice start to the weekend. Maybe he'd even get a round of golf in tomorrow.

First things first, he thought. *Let's enjoy the day and this weather.* He reached up and patted the dash of the plane's control panel. "My little plane, my little adventure. Life is good," he said to no one as he looked out the side window.

As he and his plane cruised down the coast on what was supposed to be a leisurely, short, two-hour flight, Steve Adams had no possible clue that his destination, as well as his life, would be forever altered by forces that he could never imagine.

* * *

"Not a bad haul boys," Richard said as he looked in the catch bin located in the back of the boat. "Looks like we've got some Sea Bass, a couple Trout and even a couple good size Flounder. Gonna be some good eating later on! What say we pull in these lines and start heading back in?"

In concert, Traise and Johnny both stood up from their seats. "Sounds good to us," they called out as they each grabbed a pole and began reeling in the lines.

"Maybe we should check on Sam again," Traise said with a snicker.

Johnny laughed. "Yeah, he's been asleep since we got here. Think he enjoyed the trip?"

Richard stepped over to the door which accessed the below deck quarters that contained a "U" shaped sleeping area as well as portable toilet and kitchenette. He leaned down and turned the handle which opened the small compartment door. "Yo, Sam, still alive in there?"

Sam lifted his head and squinted as the sunlight suddenly lit up the space. "We home yet?"

"Not quite, brother," Richard said. "Packing up now and heading back in a few minutes. Should be at the marina in about an hour or so. You gonna make it?"

Lying on his side, Sam lifted up on one elbow. "I do believe I shall survive. But if you think I'm coming out here again tomorrow, you are sadly mistaken, sir. Wake me up when I can stand on solid ground or there's a liquor store in sight, whichever comes first."

Richard laughed, "You got it. Before you know it, we'll be at Chatties sampling some of Laura's famous Orange Crushes."

Richard closed the door and stood up with a grin on his face while shaking his head, "Sam said he's not coming tomorrow."

Traise and Johnny gave each other a quizzical look. "Have a hard time believing that," Johnny said sarcastically.

"Right?" said Traise with a chuckle. "I would've bet money that he'd be chomping at the bit to get back out here."

The three finished reeling in the lines and then secured the fishing gear before Richard had Traise head back to the bow to pull up the anchor. Looking up into the early afternoon sky, Richard said in his captain's voice, "Good timing. Looks like some clouds are starting to come in. Didn't think the weather was supposed to turn, but it's better to be safe than sorry."

Then he returned to his old-buddy tone. "Plus I've got to wash this thing down before we go to the bar."

* * *

After flying for just over an hour and reaching the Chesapeake Bay Bridge Tunnel located just south of Cape Charles, Virginia, Steve Adams made a slow bank to the right until he was heading north once again. The flight so far had been just what he anticipated: stress-free and relaxing. He adjusted his northbound course a bit closer to land so he could observe the multiple small seaside towns and beaches that peppered the landscape of the Eastern Shore. Unlike the high-activity area of Ocean City, the lower shore was a picture of solitude with its laid-back, not-in-a-hurry style of living. He knew that it was only a matter of time until the area succumbed to the pressures of expansion, development, and modernization. Hopefully, it wouldn't be for a number of years, but he knew it was inevitable.

As he looked out to his left, he noticed what looked like a small weather front approaching the coast from the ocean. "That's a bit strange," he said to himself. "The weather reports had no mention of anything today."

One of the most important things he always did prior to flying was to check the flight conditions because no pilot ever wanted to be caught in adverse weather. Although he had plenty of flight hours, he didn't feel comfortable when flying in, or even near, the smallest storm. He shrugged off his concern, though, as he only had another hour or so in the air. "Probably just a small, early summer squall," he spoke aloud into the crisp echo of the small cabin, hearing more confidence in his voice than he felt in his mind. "I can just go around or above it if needed."

Chapter Two

Annie Hartman pushed the key into the lock and turned it to the left. She heard the familiar click of the deadbolt retreating as she turned the knob to open the front door to her home. It had been a long day at Darcy's Place, a quaint little restaurant in the southern Pennsylvania hamlet of Hyndman. She worked the breakfast and lunch shift, arriving at work at 5 a.m. and not getting off until just after two. Waitress work could be exhausting, especially during these summer days when business picked up. She was glad to be back in the peaceful confines of her small, two-bedroom house.

Annie placed her keys on the kitchen counter, kicked off her white sneakers, and called out, "Hannah, where you at girl?" Almost immediately, she heard the sound of little paws scrambling against the hardwood floor from the bedroom. A few seconds later, the little white dog rushed around the corner to the kitchen, tail wagging excitedly because "Mom" was home. As she did every day when she came home, the small terrier rushed up to Annie, stood on her back legs, and put her front paws on Annie's knees, waiting for the head rub she always enjoyed.

Annie had adopted the small terrier two years ago after seeing her picture on the internet page for the local shelter. When she first saw the photo, something in those small brown eyes drew Annie to her. She visited the shelter and was told by the staff that Animal Control had turned in the dog they named Hannah after she was found in a run-down back yard of a local residence. Although it couldn't be proven, they relayed that it was likely the animal had been abused. Hannah was quite timid and would cower anytime a person would reach out to touch or pet her. When Annie stepped inside the small kennel for the first time, she sat down and put her hand out to the pup that was backed into a corner, shaking. At first, Hannah looked sheepishly to the side and didn't respond to Annie's voice. After just a minute or two and with more calming words, Hannah made eye contact and slowly inched closer. She cautiously sniffed the outreached hand, looked up at Annie, and then crawled up and into her lap, snuggling her head on Annie's arm. From that moment on, the two had been constant companions. Both had endured hardships in their lives, and the comfort and joy they gave each other made every day a bit more bearable.

After the welcoming, Annie opened the refrigerator and took out a plate of leftovers. She placed the dish in the microwave, pushed a few buttons, and watched the plate begin to rotate.

"Whatcha think, Hannah?" Annie said. "Feel like a little baked ham and potatoes for dinner?"

Hannah sat anxiously at her feet, tail still wagging and eyes wide open. When the timer went off, Annie grabbed the plate, some silverware, and a glass of wine and headed to the living room with Hannah following closely behind. Once the simple but somewhat satisfying meal had been consumed (with Hannah getting a bit more people food than usual), Annie took the plate back to the kitchen and placed it and the utensils in the dishwasher.

Then Annie turned back to the counter. "Guess it's time to see what the mailman brought us today, huh girl?" She picked up the small stack of envelopes she had previously taken out of the mailbox on the front door and shuffled through them, looking at the address on each to determine what was junk and what she should open. After the third envelope, she stopped and stared at a smaller white envelope about the size of a thank-you card. Annie placed the other envelopes on the counter, went to the living room, and sat down in the small recliner by the fireplace. Hannah jumped up and curled around on her lap. Annie gently patted her on the head and let out a small sigh. "That time again, Hannah," she said as she opened the envelope, unfolded the card, and began reading.

Inside the envelope was the same note she received around this time of year for the past thirty-five years. It was an invitation to attend the annual memorial service for the crew of the Coast Guard Cutter Tuckahoma. The ship and crew, including her husband, Seaman Josh Hartman, had been lost at sea in 1983. Eight months after they were secretly married, Josh had deployed on a routine sixty-day patrol to the Caribbean, never to return. It was a mystery that had yet to be solved. After the largest search-and-rescue operation ever conducted by the Coast Guard and Navy, no trace of the ship had ever been found. Annie, along with all the other family members of the crew would forever wonder about the details and ultimate fate of their loved ones.

Her life had changed from that point on as she mourned the loss of her love. To compound her loss, Annie had planned to tell her husband when he returned from the patrol that she was pregnant with his son. She named him Josh Jr., in honor of her fallen hero. The young J.J., as he was called, grew up the spitting image of his father and, against her adamant objections, joined the Navy in 2001 when he was eighteen only to also, unimaginably, be lost at sea while underway two years later. The pyramid of tragedies was sometimes too much for her to bear. Somehow and some way, she gathered strength from their memory and continued on. Now fifty-three years old, Annie never let herself become involved in another serious relationship. Her heart had been broken too many times to consider loving again.

She lifted Hannah up from her lap and placed her on the floor as she stood up from the recliner and walked to the fireplace. Reaching up, she opened the lid of a small wooden box on the mantel and placed the invitation atop the thirty-four others inside. She then reached over to the framed photos that were just a few inches away and gently touched the face of her husband and then, just as slowly, touched the picture of her son. Her eyes welled up and a small trickle of tears began streaming down her face. "I miss you both so very much. Wherever you are, know that I will love you forever," Annie said. Then she returned to the recliner, let Hannah nestle on her lap again, closed her eyes, and drifted off to sleep.

* * *

The dream was always the same. Annie found herself floating on an unknown body of water, alone in a small boat surrounded by a heavy fog. There was no sound except the gentle lapping of water against the side of the boat. She would look forward into misty nothingness with a feeling of anxiety but no fear.

Gradually, she would notice that the fog seemed to be thinning in front of her as the sky slowly began to lighten. She could hear what sounded like muffled voices in the distance but couldn't make out exactly what was being said. As she continued drifting, the outline of people began to appear in front of her, and the voices started to become clearer. She could make out laughter and excited chatter and could now see two figures standing on what looked like a pier, waving in an encouraging manner toward her. Her anxiety continued to grow as the boat drifted slowly toward them and the fog continued to dissipate.

A smile began to form on her face and her heart began beating faster as she saw her husband Josh, along with her son J.J. on the pier, waving their arms as if trying to get her attention. They were both standing underneath a large wooden, hand-painted sign that spanned the end of the pier between two tall wooden beams. In bold orange letters, the sign spelled out one word: Athanasia. Annie and her boat continued the last few feet to the pier as Josh and J.J. both bent down toward her. Her husband held out his hand to pull her up from the boat and just as they were about to touch …

Annie's eyes snapped open with the loud triple knock on the door as Hannah let out a startled bark. Annie shook her head quickly side to side, clearing the effects of the dream from her mind, and stood up from the recliner and walked to the front door. Upon opening, she found a smiling Bo Davidson on the step facing her. "One cream and two sugars?" Bo said as he held up one cup of the steaming convenience store coffee towards Annie.

She took the hot beverage from him and with a small laugh said, "Same as every day, Bo. Come on in."

Annie met Bo a few years earlier through a mutual friend at a cookout and hit it off with him right away. Bo was from Bedford, which was twenty minutes from her hometown of Hyndman, Pennsylvania. The two towns had always been bitter rivals during their high school years, and rarely did the student populations intertwine. But as those days faded, so did the competition aspect.

Bo moved closer to Hyndman five years ago when he found a farm and acreage for sale just outside town in the small village of Buffalo Mills. The attraction of the land, with its farmhouse, barn, and small stream running through the property was exactly what he had been looking for. He had retired at a somewhat early age from the railroad and his plan was to enjoy the solitude and country setting that the farm offered. His days were spent fishing, hunting, or just piddling around fixing up the homestead. The only thing missing was somebody to share his life with.

When Bo met Annie, he was immediately attracted to her. They had spent quite a few days together either on the farm, going to the various festivals in the area or just hanging out. When he passed through Hyndman, he sometimes stopped by her place to check on her and see how she was doing. If he had his way, the relationship would be more than just as friends, but he understood Annie's past and her reluctance to go any further. For now, he would be satisfied with being with her as much as he could without applying pressure for any type of commitment. He loved her and would do anything he could for her anytime she asked. Annie knew how he felt and was always conscious of his emotions. She always made sure that she never did anything to lead him on or take advantage of him. The hurt and heartbreak of her past were still too strong, and she was not yet able to let the wall surrounding her show any cracks. Maybe someday, but for now, it was what it was.

As they sat down at the kitchen table, Bo noticed that Annie seemed a bit unsettled.

"Another dream?" he said as he took a sip of his coffee.

"Yeah," she said. "Got another invitation in the mail today. Seems like every time the dreams get further apart, something happens to start them up again. It's okay, I'll be fine." She paused for just a second and changed the subject. "So, what's on your agenda today?"

Bo took another sip and said, "Not much. Came in to get some things for my water wheel project I'm putting in the stream. But you know what? Got an idea. How about we take a few hours and hit up the blueberry festival this afternoon? Might take your mind off of things for a little bit."

Annie looked at him with a light smile. She knew what he was trying to do and loved that he always tried to cheer her up when she was a little down. "That sounds pretty good. Why don't you go get your supplies and pick me up in an hour? That'll give me a chance to freshen up and get this restaurant smell off of me."

Bo stood, came to attention, and saluted her. "Your wish is my command, Ma'am." Then he turned and walked toward the door. "Don't put too much work into getting ready. Those farm boys will be staring at you as it is."

Annie laughed as he exited. "Yeah, right. I'll try to keep it toned down." She pulled the

screened door shut, shook her head, and chuckled. As she watched him walk toward the street,
she said to herself, "That guy is something else."

* * *

It had been just a few minutes since Steve
Adams had first observed the clouds off to the
left of his plane as he flew back up the coast towards Ocean City. At first, the small weather
front appeared non-threatening, and he remained on his course and was now about three
miles off shore from the small fishing village of
Wachapreague, Virginia. Steve started to become
a bit more concerned as he could see flashes of
light inside the area, which indicated to him that
the front was possibly turning into a thunder-
storm. "Just what I needed," he said as he continued to eye the area.

The front seemed to be approaching the
coast and his position faster now, and he knew
he had to decide which way to deal with the approaching problem. He could adjust course
closer to the beach, but that wouldn't guarantee
the storm wouldn't still blow in on top of him.
His only comfortable option would be to climb
in altitude and attempt to get above the squall.

With his decision made, he slowly pulled
back on the plane's yoke and started a gradual

ascent to five thousand feet. *This should take me above that mess,* he thought as he monitored the altimeter with the number on the display clicking upward.

As the plane began to climb, he felt a knot forming in his stomach as a slight uneasiness started to creep over him. *I hate bad weather,* he thought. Even with his experience, he knew that while flying, weather was unpredictable and could be your worst nightmare if you weren't ready and able to deal with it. He had to trust his judgment and his years of flying to ensure that his nice, relaxing, summer day flight would not turn into a test of his abilities as a pilot. The area off to his left continued to darken, and the flashes of light inside were becoming more intense. He felt the effects of the increasing wind on the plane as he continued upward. "I'm not liking this at all. Not one little bit," he said to himself as his grip on the yoke handle became tighter and more pronounced.

* * *

As Richard continued to navigate the fishing boat on a westerly course towards Chincoteague, Traise stood beside him but kept looking back towards Blackfish Banks and the storm, which was rapidly increasing in size and intensity.

"I thought you looked at the weather report this morning," he said loudly to Richard trying to be heard over the increased decibels of the twin engines as they were now at full throttle.

"I did and there was nothing about any storms. You think I want to be caught in a rainstorm out here?" Richard said as he looked over his shoulder to see the fast-approaching front. "Hopefully we can outrun it and get into the marina before it hits us."

Traise looked back at Richard and sensed a little apprehension in his friend's voice and demeanor. "You got this, bro. But if you don't and we get soaked, guess who's buying all the rounds later on?" he said as he smiled and patted Richard on the shoulder.

Richard again glanced over his shoulder, then looked back with raised eyebrows at Traise. "Ha! Like you ever bought a round of drinks in your life," he said with a wink. "Better check on Sam and Gendo to see how they're doing. And make sure there's nothing loose on the deck. It's starting to get a little choppy, and we don't need anything flying around if it gets any worse."

Traise opened the berthing compartment door and peered in to see Gendo sprawled out on one side of the cushioned area sound asleep and Sam on the other clinging to a bucket with one hand and grasping the countertop with the other.

Looking at Traise through heavy eyes, Sam mumbled, "What's with the bouncing around all of a sudden?" He wiped the sweat from his face with his t-shirt.

"Just a little increase in the waves, nothing to worry about," Traise replied. "Wanted to check to see how you were making out in here."

Sam looked down at the bucket. "Just get me back to land." Then he looked up at Traise and said half-heartedly, "And let it be known that if you ever attempt to talk me into getting back on a boat again, any and all friendship agreements between us will be terminated immediately."

Traise reached over and rubbed the top of his friend's head. "Hang in there, Buddy. Won't be long and we'll have you back on terra firma in no time."

Traise then shifted his attention. "Wake up Gendo!" he said as he shook Johnny's leg on the other side.

Gendo opened his eyes. "Are we in already?" he said as he yawned and stretched out his arms.

"Geesh, what is it with you two?" Traise said. "No, we're not in already. We might be getting some rough weather, so get up and help me tie things down out here."

Gendo looked quizzically at Traise. "Rough weather? What kind of rough weather? I thought it was supposed to be nice all day?"

Traise frowned at him. "Yeah, we all did. Come on and give me a hand."

Johnny looked over at Sam and said, "You coming?"

Sam raised his wobbly head and said sarcastically, "What do *you* think?"

Gendo looked at Sam, then Traise, and then Sam again and said, "My guess would be no," as he slowly got upright. "All right Traise, let's go. Just show me what to do."

* * *

After reaching five thousand feet and leveling off, Steve Adams found that the maneuver hadn't taken him above the storm, which was now less than half a mile off his left wing and closing fast. The attitude indicator was becoming more and more erratic with the increasing wind. Also called the Artificial Horizon, the gauge showed the aircraft's relation to the horizon. From this, Steve could tell whether the wings were level and if the nose of the plane was pointing above or below the horizon.

Steve knew that if he couldn't avoid the storm and ended up inside of it, the downdrafts and updrafts would cause havoc with a plane this size. The changes in air pressure and severity could push an aircraft around like a kid's toy. With the increased turbulence, he had to continually push and pull on the yoke to maintain the pitch of the plane and, at the same time, turn the control left and right to manage the roll and stay level.

"Guess I should have turned to the coast earlier," he said out loud. What first appeared just ten minutes ago as a small summer squall had blossomed into what had become a dangerous system increasing in width as well as height. Steve hadn't thought the storm would come up on him as quickly as it had, and his lapse in judgment and not altering his course found him in a precarious situation. With his attention almost exclusively on his instruments, he didn't notice that the outward band of the storm was now not only to his left but also extending in front of him. The sky, which was so bright and beautiful earlier, had become eerily dark, and rain started to pelt the aircraft sounding like BB's hitting the wings. He switched on the windshield wipers and reached for the straps of his harness, giving a sharp pull on both sides of his chest securing him tightly into the seat.

"Better buckle up," he announced. "Looks like it's going to be a bumpy ride."

* * *

Richard pulled back on the throttle controls of the engines as the waves continued to increase in size while visibility became limited with the downpour of rain. Although they were making headway, the water had begun to churn with four to five-foot whitecaps. The wind was whipping and swirling around the thirty-foot vessel, and the combination of waves and wind were making it increasingly difficult to maintain course. The experience of being a small boat coxswain in the Coast Guard gave Richard a huge advantage in piloting a boat in these types of conditions. The one big difference and of major concern to him was that Coast Guard boats were built for adverse weather. The Grady White was not, and, although the sturdy vessel was holding up just fine to this point, the pounding it was taking had him concerned. As a precaution, he had instructed the other three to put on lifejackets. The he asked Traise take the helm temporarily so he could don his.

They were all under the canopy now, holding on as the boat pitched up and from side to side with the onslaught of the erratic waves. Richard watched for waves coming towards them from each side and adjusted accordingly so the vessel wasn't swamped or, even worse, over-turned. Lightning flashed all around, and the large claps of thunder caused them all to flinch downward simultaneously. With all that was going on, not one word was uttered between them. The situation had become tense and Traise, Gendo, and Sam knew that Richard had his hands full and didn't need distractions him from his concentration.

"Son of a bitch, the GPS just went out!" Richard said loudly. Traise looked at his buddy and saw that Richard seemed to be more pissed than afraid.

"So, what does that mean?" Traise yelled to him.

Without changing expression, Richard explained in terse words, "That means we can't tell where we're at or where we're going. The compass is all over the place too."

Traise turned his head towards Gendo and Sam, and he could see that his two friends were becoming increasingly afraid of the situation that they found themselves in. He winked and gave a thumbs-up sign in an attempt to relay some confidence to them that they would be okay. He hoped they believed him, but their eyes indicated that he wasn't very successful. He wasn't entirely convinced himself right now as the ever-intensifying storm totally engulfed the boat.

* * *

The definition of Spatial Disorientation is, "The inability of a person to determine his true body position, motion, and altitude relative to the earth or his surroundings." Pilots and divers are susceptible to this phenomenon as it affects their mental state to the point that, although they are convinced they are in one place or position, they are actually in another.

As the situation in the plane deteriorated, pilot Steve Adams had slowly succumbed to a classic case of Spatial Distortion as he continued to fly. All of the instruments on the plane's control panel were wildly fluctuating, and visibility had become almost non-existent within the dark clouds, lightning, and heavy rain. The airspeed indicator, compass, and attitude indicator had all inexplicably gone haywire in the weather system that surrounded him. Without his instrument readings, his instincts and experience told him, although he was being buffeted about, he was still on a good general course and at a safe altitude.

Steve had absolutely no idea that for the past few minutes, he and his plane had been on a downward path and was only five hundred feet above the turbulent surface of the ocean. In less than a minute, the plane would hit the water at over one hundred miles per hour. His chances of surviving were minimal, and even if he did, the possibility of severe injury during the crash and eventual drowning appeared to be the most plausible outcome to his once-relaxing weekend.

* * *

The wind, rain, and waves crashing against the boat made it impossible for any of the four aboard to see or hear the sound of the approaching aircraft that was on a direct collision course with them. It was too late for Richard to respond when the plane burst through the heavy clouds and rain, clipping the antennas on top of the vessel, ripping them from their mounts, and throwing debris into the air. The detached wiring was left whipping in the gusting wind.

The four stunned friends looked on in horror as the small plane made a sudden surge upward with a simultaneous sharp bank to the left. The maneuver was so drastic and at such a low level that the left wing tip dug into the waves and pirouetted the plane into the water with such force that the wing was torn from the fuselage. The aircraft stood up on its nose for just an instant, then came slamming down on its underbelly into the turbulent sea. The prop from the engine cut wildly into the water before disinte-grating, sending shards of steel in all directions. Smoke poured into the cockpit as waves hit the hot metal of the now disabled engine.

"Holy shit!" a shocked Traise yelled as the plane came to rest on the ocean's surface only four hundred feet away from the boat. "Where the hell did that come from?"

Richard couldn't answer right away as he was trying to maintain control of the vessel while staring in disbelief at the downed plane. Instinc-tively, he yelled "Hang on!" and yanked the wheel of the boat hard to the right, sending it lurching toward the plane.

* * *

Only quick reflexes saved Steve Adams from plowing into the vessel that suddenly appeared directly in front of his plane. In a split second, he pulled the yoke back as hard as possible in an attempt to gain altitude and avoid the collision. The sudden upward pull inadvertently caused him to turn the control to the left, which caused the aircraft to roll hard to that side. With no time to compensate, the left wing tore into the water, causing the plane to cartwheel downward nose first into the torrent.

Steve's head slammed into the left window, dazing him almost to the point of blacking out. The left door of the plane ripped from the fuselage and the windshield shattered from pieces of the propeller that had exploded when it tore into the water. Water began to pour into the cabin as he struggled to maintain consciousness.

With the plane coming to rest in the water and upright for now, Steve attempted to undo his safety harness, knowing that he had to get out as quickly as possible. Only when he tried to raise his right arm and felt the excruciating pain did he realize that a shard of metal from the propeller had lodged into his triceps, making his arm unusable. Fading in and out, he desperately kept trying to free himself from the restraints as the water level continued to rise in the cockpit.

With all his remaining strength, he used his left hand and pulled the harness off his left shoulder, not realizing that the lap portion and the right shoulder harness were still intact. His struggle began to fade quickly, as did his level of awareness. *Oh my god ... I'm going to die,* he thought as he slumped forward and lapsed into darkness.

* * *

In his state of unconsciousness, Steve didn't feel the hard tug on his harness and the pair of hands pulling on him. He had no way of knowing that the hands found and pushed the quick release mechanism, releasing him from his confinement. In an instant, another set of hands grabbed him and pulled him from the cockpit and into the water surrounding the plane.

"We've got him!" Traise yelled as he and Gendo struggled against the waves and rain to get away from the rapidly sinking plane, each swimming with one arm as they towed the pilot towards the boat.

"Keep his head above water, and I'll get as close as I can!" Richard yelled back as he maneuvered the boat towards the three. "Sam, grab that life-ring and toss it to them when I tell you to!" Richard increased the throttle and turned the wheel to come around. "I'll block the waves as best as I can, but I'll only be able to hold it for a few seconds, so make your throw count!" he instructed.

As the boat continued to toss about, Sam staggered to the stern and pulled the life-ring from its holder. He was trying to maintain his balance and fought to keep any remaining contents in his stomach. As Richard slowly brought the boat to within ten yards of the three in the water, he yelled, "Now Sam, Now!"

Taking a deep breath and using a sideways motion, Sam threw the life-ring, the rope line feeding out as it flew towards Traise, Gendo, and the injured pilot. The throw was well left of the trio, but, luckily, the wind blew the ring back towards them and landed just a few feet from Traise's outreached arm.

"Got it!" Traise yelled as he grabbed onto the ring with his one free arm.

"Pull them in, Sam!" Richard bellowed as he continued to fight the waves against the boat. He put the engines into neutral, stopping the props from spinning. "Bring'em to the ladder at the stern!"

Sam had already started to reel in the rope once he saw Traise grab onto it. In just a few seconds, he had pulled all three close enough to the boat for Traise to grab hold of the ladder and yell, "I've got him! Gendo, get on board first so you can help Sam pull this guy up!"

With a nod of his head, Gendo climbed up the rungs of the ladder while still being hit by waves, rain, and wind. Once on board, he and Sam reached down and, at peak wave height, grabbed the unconscious and limp pilot under each arm and pulled him onto the stern of the boat. Then they each turned their attention to Traise who was still in the water clinging to the ladder. As before, they waited just a second until a wave elevated him close enough for them to latch onto him and pull him on board as well.

As they all lay on the deck exhausted from what they had just accomplished, Richard kicked the engines back in gear and yelled, "Nice job, boys! Now take him below out of this weather. Looks like he's bleeding pretty good there on his arm. There's a first-aid kit in there, so pull that out and get him patched up the best you can."

* * *

Within a few minutes and with a massive headache and his right arm bandaged, Steve Adams slowly opened his eyes and peered up at the faces staring back at him. More than slightly groggy, he looked at all three and quietly said, "Are you from the boat?"

Traise, Sam, and Gendo looked at each other and then back to their new passenger. "That's us," they said in unison.

Traise finished securing the bandage on Steve's arm and continued, "Nice bump on your head you got there, and you're going to need to see a doctor for that arm. But for now, sit tight and try to relax. Oh, and the guy that owns this boat has a question for you."

Steve looked up at his rescuers. "What's that?" he said, trying to stay awake.

"He wants to know if your airplane insurance covers boat damage, Traise said with a
chuckle.

Chapter Three

The sun was setting and dusk quickly approaching as Bo and Annie arrived back at her house following their outing to the festival. They enjoyed a wonderful day of walking around looking at the various crafts and blueberry themed items offered throughout the outdoor venue. The weather had been great and the food amazing with an almost unlimited choice of everything blueberry. If something could be made with the fruit, it was there. Some delicious, some not so much. Annie had to laugh when Bo decided to take a chance and sample the "Breakfast on a Stick," which consisted of a slice of pork belly covered with blueberry-infused pancake batter, deep fried, and then drizzled with blueberry syrup. "Nope, nope, nope," he said after forcing the bite down. "That's just not right," he murmured as he walked quickly but calmly to the nearest trash container, not wanting to offend the vendor. They spent the rest of their time sampling more traditional offerings like cakes, pies, jams, and jellies with much more appealing results.

"Home safe and sound," Bo said as he put the truck into park.

Annie looked at him. "Thank you so much, Bo. It was a great day that I really needed to take my mind off of things."

Bo smiled back at her and gently touched her hand. "Any day I get to spend time with a beautiful lady is a good day. Can I walk you to the door?"

Annie leaned over and kissed him on the cheek. "I'm good, but thank you. I'm going to feed Hannah, take a shower, and go to bed. Got to get up early for work you know."

Bo gave a faux-disappointed look to her. "Can't blame a guy for trying, can ya?" he said as he squeezed her hand again.

Annie pulled the door handle and stepped out of the truck. When she shut the door, she leaned into the cab with a smile. "Keep trying. You never know when I might surprise you," she said with a mischievous grin.

Bo raised his eyebrows at her statement, put his foot on the brake, and shifted the truck into drive. "Challenge accepted, my dear," he said with a devilish half smile. "I'll call you in a day or two to see how you're doing," he continued as he lifted off the brake and began to pull away.

"I know you will," Annie said to him as she gave a little wave and stood back as the truck began to move. She stood for just a few seconds watching Bo drive away thinking to herself, *Such a good man.* She then turned and walked up the concrete walkway, pulled open the screened door, and unlocked the main door. She was ready for a good night's sleep, but, deep down, she knew that the past was about to visit her once again.

* * *

The rain and wind had finally subsided, and the sea was calming down, giving the five men in the boat a much-needed reprieve from the beating they had just endured. Steve Adams, along with Sam and Gendo, slept below as Traise and Richard sat in the captain's chairs on deck, both exhausted. They had been taking turns at the helm throughout the storm, and now both just sat still, silently embracing the quiet that had arrived as quickly as the storm did. A few minutes earlier, Richard had cut the engines to save fuel and now the worn out boat was drifting with only the sound of small waves lapping against the hull.

Without looking up, Traise said slowly, "Well, that was fun."

Richard shrugged his shoulders slightly. "You have a much different definition of fun than I do." He looked up and glanced around the boat. "The old girl held up, though. I had some serious concerns there for a while, but we made it through. You and Gendo did a hell of a job getting that guy out of the plane. He was a goner if you hadn't pulled him out."

Traise looked up and out at the water surrounding them and said with a sigh, "Right place at the right time, I guess. So now what?"

Richard reached up to the console and tapped on the plastic cover of the compass. "Well, the compass still isn't working, GPS is out, and the plane took our antennae, so we've got no radio." Looking up at the sky, he continued, "And, with the cloud cover still here, I have no idea what direction to head. Unless another boat comes by or the clouds lift, we're pretty much dead in the water for now."

Traise reached into his pocket, took out his cell phone, and looked at the words *no service* on the screen. "Well, this is useless out here."

Richard pulled his phone out and observed the same message. "Same here," he said with disgust as he tossed the phone into the storage bin on the console. "Guess we'll sit tight for a while until the clouds lift."

Traise looked at his lifelong friend and said with a half-smile, "Did you ever see Gilligan's Island?"

Richard gave a mild chuckle. "Yeah, but instead of Ginger and Maryann, we've got Sam, Gendo, and some pilot guy."

Traise rose from the chair and made his way to one of the coolers that had been tied down and secured, opened the lid, took out two beers, and tossed one to Richard. "I think we both deserve one of these."

Richard caught the bottle, twisted the cap off, and held it up to Traise as if giving a toast. "Here's to us, brother. A storm about sank us, a plane nearly took us out, we saved a guy from drowning, and now we're having a cold beer. Doesn't get any better than this, huh?"

Traise raised his beer back towards Richard, and they both took a long swig from their bottles. Traise made his way back to the chair, sank into his seat, and said sarcastically, "Let's hope not."

* * *

The sound of the copper teapot whistling on the stove had reached its apex when Annie took it off the burner and poured the piping-hot water into the cup. She liked to finish off her day with some green tea, which, for whatever reason, always relaxed her. After arriving home from the festival, she fed Hannah the usual half cup of kibble with a few warmed chicken gizzards and then took a hot shower while her little white companion devoured the small bowl of food. As she was drying off, she heard light scratching on the bathroom door, which was the signal from Hannah that she had finished eating, and it was now time for one final trip outside before they both went to bed.

Annie wrapped the towel around her body, tucked one end into the top, and opened the door. "Just like clockwork," she said. As soon as the door opened, the small terrier bolted from a sitting position toward the back door and stood somewhat patiently with her tail wagging, waiting for the screened door to open. Annie unlocked the door and pushed open the entry into the backyard. There was no hesitation as Hannah burst through the opening and ran out into the evening.

Annie pulled the door closed and returned to the kitchen to retrieve her tea that had been steeping while she showered. They both had their timing down to almost the second, so Annie knew it would be about fifteen minutes before Hannah returned to the door to come back inside. She grabbed the cup of tea and walked to the living room, picked up the remote, and turned the television on to catch the evening news. Then she placed the cup of tea on the coaster that was on the side table and plunked down onto the plush recliner.

The day had been a good one, and she smiled as she sipped the tea and replayed the experience at the festival with Bo. He had a way of always making her feel comfortable and secure and never failed to make her laugh. Even during her low points, Bo could lift her up with some saying or mannerism to make everything better, albeit temporarily. She looked up at the picture of her husband Josh on the mantel and whispered to herself, "Why can't I let go?" A tear formed in the corner of her eye as she continued to peer at the photo.

The moment was broken when she heard the anticipated scratching on the back door. She wiped her eye and set the cup back on the coaster. She stood up from the recliner and walked to the door, pushing it lightly to open and stepped to the side as Hannah darted back in. As she returned to the living room, she heard the news anchor state that the Coast Guard had initiated a search for a small plane with only a pilot on board that was overdue from Ocean City, Maryland. She watched the report and shook her head. She understood all too well what the family and friends of the pilot were feeling and going through. *Prayers for you, and I hope you're okay,* she thought.

She turned the television off, took her cup to the kitchen, and placed it in the sink. "Okay Baby girl, it's been a long day. Time to go to bed," she said to her companion. With her tail wagging, Hannah didn't hesitate and trotted towards the bedroom. Annie followed her and, after removing the towel, donned the oversized t-shirt she always wore to bed, pulled back the covers, and slipped in between the sheets. Hannah beat her to the punch and had already jumped onto the comforter and waited until Annie got settled. Then she lightly laid down with her head on Annie's shoulder and they both drifted quickly off to sleep.

* * *

In her dream, the air was quiet as Annie's small vessel drifted slowly toward the dock with only the same single passenger sitting alone on board. Annie felt the anticipation well up as she saw the same two figures standing on the wooden pier watching her approach. Both smiled as the boat crept forward. In her dream state, Annie knew what would happen next, just as it had so many times before. She would wake up just as her husband Josh reached out to her.

However, this time, instead of kneeling down and reaching out to her, Josh remained standing alongside her son J.J. and slowly lifted his arm and pointed to the sky behind her. Annie turned her head around slowly in the direction that Josh was directing and saw a fully lit moon shining brightly. When she turned back around, she saw nothing. Not only were Josh and J.J. gone, but the wooden structure had also disappeared. Her anticipation turned to confusion as she quickly looked all around, seeing nothing but the sea and sky surrounding her.

Her eyes popped open, and she looked to see the alarm clock on the nightstand showing it was exactly midnight. She then turned back and saw Hannah sleeping beside her. Her little friend had managed to get under the blanket with only her head visible on the other pillow, looking so quiet and content, without a care in the world. Annie stroked the dog's head gently and rolled over, took a deep breath, and fell back asleep.

* * *

The night sky was slowly clearing as the boat drifted aimlessly with her five passengers on board. Traise and Richard were still in the cabin seats but asleep as exhaustion had overtaken the two, granting them a well-deserved reprieve for the previous few hours.

But then they were both suddenly jolted awake by a rough, gravelly voice that came out of nowhere. "Ahoy there, everything okay on board?"

Both men simultaneously sat upright and looked around to find the origin of the call. When they trained their eyes off the starboard side and about thirty yards away, they saw an older man sitting at the back of a small wooden skiff with one hand on the throttle arm of an outboard motor. He was looking at them. His worn vessel had seen better days with the paint faded from the hull and no registration numbers visible.

The old man waved to them with a back and forth hand motion and yelled again. "Noticed that you had no lights on and wanted to check to see if you all were good!"

Traise and Richard looked at each other, then back to the old man. Richard waved and yelled back, "Actually, ran into a bit of trouble during the storm. Navigation and radio are out, and we've got an injured man on board who needs medical attention."

The man, dressed only in raggedy shorts and a faded Hawaiian shirt, slowly guided his boat closer to them. "Looks like your boat's a little worse for wear as well," he said as he glanced at the remnants of the antennas that were dangling loosely from the top of their boat. "Will she fire up?" he asked.

"She should, but we're getting low on fuel," Richard said as he nodded in the affirmative.

"Give her a try," the old man said as he continued to maneuver the small boat off to the side of them. Richard took a few steps to the console, grabbed the key, and turned it to the right. The twin engines cranked a few times and turned over with a low rumble. Richard then turned back to the old man and gave a thumbs-up sign.

With the engines now running, the old man talked a bit louder to be heard. "It'll take about twenty minutes, but follow me," he said as he began to turn his boat slowly away from them. He then turned the throttle control, and the small outboard began to sputter as the propeller took hold in the glass-like water. He looked back over his shoulder, yelled again with a grin, "And try to keep up!"

With the sound of the engines starting, Sam and Gendo emerged out from the lower compartment and joined Traise and Richard on deck. "What's going on?" Gendo said as Richard took the helm, put the engines in gear, and began to turn the craft to follow the skiff.

Traise shrugged his shoulders while watching the old man in the small boat slowly move away from them. "Guy just showed up out of nowhere and said to follow him."

With a look of confusion, Sam turned to Richard. "And we're going to follow him? Where too?"

Richard increased the power slightly, slowly turned his head from side to side, and said, "No idea. But we have no choice right now. We've got no navigation and no radio. With the storm and then us drifting for a while, I've got no clue where we are. Wherever he's taking us, it can't be too far away if he's out here in that little thing."

As they all continued to watch the small boat in front of them, Traise touched Gendo on the shoulder. "How's our patient doing?"

Without looking away from the old man in the boat, Gendo nodded. "He's been out the whole time, but I checked on him a lot and he's breathing okay. Think he got his bell rung pretty good."

True to the old man's estimate, in about fifteen minutes, the four above deck could see a small glow of light directly ahead of the old man and his boat that was sputtering along a hundred yards or so in front of them. An outline of a pier slowly emerged through the darkness as Richard pulled back on the throttle slightly. The old man had maneuvered his skiff alongside the rickety wooden structure, pulling up closer to the shore and allowing the Grady White room enough to dock behind him. He was already on the pier waiting as Richard eased the bow towards one of the wooden pilings.

"Throw me your bow line when you're ready, and then you can pull back to secure the stern," the old man instructed.

Traise was already at the bow with the line ready to toss it over to the old man as soon as Richard directed him to.

"Go ahead, Traise. Gendo get the stern line ready!" Richard said loudly. Hearing that, Traise flung the line upwards and toward the old man, who grabbed it effortlessly and made a loop in the middle. He put the loop over the pilling while keeping hold of the end, allowing him to feed out the line as Richard slowly backed down, turned the wheel, and let the stern slowly come around to the dock. When the stern slowly bumped the dock, the old man made a few more loops or half hitches in the bow line and pulled the line taut. He then made his way back to the stern, and Gendo tossed the back line to him. As before, he slipped a loop over the pilling, applied a couple more half hitches, and secured the stern.

With the boat tied up securely, Richard turned the key, cut the engines, and turned to the other three. "Well fellas, we're here."

Gendo piped up, "And where exactly is that?"

Richard shrugged his shoulders. "Your guess is as good as mine. But it's land, so let's get off this thing. Traise, you and Sam go get our pilot and help him up here."

As the two descended below deck, Richard and Gendo stepped up from the boat onto the wooden, semi-sturdy dock. The old man had walked to the end of the dock and picked up the lit antique kerosene lantern that had guided them in from the sea.

"Bet you boys could use a break from the water," he said as he returned to them. Still holding the lantern, he reached into his shirt pocket with his other hand and pulled out a half-smoked, half-chewed cigar, licked the unburnt end, and placed it in the right side of his mouth. He then pulled out an old Zippo lighter from his pants pocket, flicked it open, and used his thumb to flick the small wheel to ignite it. Holding the flame to the cigar, he took a few hard tokes until it was lit, snapped the top closed, and returned the lighter to his pocket.

"So who do I have the pleasure of meeting?" the old man said as he reached out to shake the hand of the two on the dock.

Richard extended his arm to reciprocate and immediately felt the power in the old man's hand as they shook. "Richard Drewer," he said. Then he nodded towards Gendo. "This is Johnny Gendo. The two below are Traise Robbins and Sam Willow. We've got another guy that we pulled out of the water after his plane crashed near us. Don't know his name yet, he took a nasty blow to the head and his arm is hurt. He really needs to get checked out if there's a doctor nearby."

The old man gave Richard a slight grin and said, "I'm sure he'll be fine once he gets off the boat."

Traise and Sam emerged from the cabin, one on each side of the pilot, assisting him as he made his way gingerly to the side of the boat next to the dock.

The old man looked down, still with the small grin, and made a slight up and down nod toward him. "Hello Mr. Adams and welcome."

The four friends and Steve Adams jerked their heads towards the old man, and Richard said in a surprised tone, "You know this guy?"

The old man reached up to his cigar with his left hand, took a long drag, removed it from his mouth, and with a noticeable twinkle in his eye said, "Not really. Let's just say I have a way of knowing things. Get him up here and let's take a look at him."

Richard, along with Gendo, Traise, and Sam, gently helped the pilot, who was still affected by the crash, up off the boat and onto the dock. Steve, still a bit groggy, looked at the old man and said, "How do you know my name?"

The old man took another puff on his cigar and said, "In due time, Mr. Adams. All in due time." He then put the kerosene lantern down and reached toward the pilot. "Let's see what we have here," he said as he placed his hands on the head of the pilot and lightly rubbed the area where the pilot's head had hit the side window of the plane. The pilots' legs partially gave out, but Traise and Sam caught him. His eyes blinked quickly, closed for a few seconds, and opened back up. He stood up straight without any assistance and looked into the eyes of the old man.

"What did you do?" Steve said as the old man now turned his attention to the injured arm. The four friends looked on in astonishment as the old man took both of his hands and placed them around the bandage on the pilot's arm, still in the makeshift sling that Traise had applied, and gently massaged the area.

"There, that should do it," he said as he reached behind the pilot's neck and untied the knot of the sling. "You won't need this thing anymore."

Steve slowly lowered his injured arm and, with his other hand, felt his arm where the shard of propeller had penetrated just hours ago and began rubbing up and down on the area, searching for the wound that was so painful just a few seconds ago. He felt his arm in amazement as he tried to find some indication of the injury.

"You can take that bandage off now too," the old man said as he turned and picked up his lantern. "Follow me, boys. We'll head up this way," he said as he began walking up the dock.

Sam, with his eyes never leaving the old man, leaned into Traise's ear and whispered, "What just happened?"

Traise turned to Sam with raised eyebrows and wide eyes, lifted his shoulders and shook his head slowly from side to side, not saying say a word.

Steve removed the last turn of the bandage and stared in amazement at his arm. No cut, no blood, no sign of anything. He bent his arm up and down without pain and again felt where the injury should have been. He looked at his four rescuers with a bewildered expression and then turned towards the old man, now getting further away from them.

The five of them began walking briskly up the dock to catch up with their host. When they were just a few feet behind him, Richard spoke up. "Excuse me, sir, but we didn't catch your name."

Without breaking his stride, the old man turned over his shoulder and said in their direction, "Last name is Hartman, Samuel Hartman. But folks around here call me 'Chief.'"

Traise sped up slightly until he was side by side with the old man. "How did you do that?" he asked, looking ahead as he spoke.

"Do what?" said the old man as he continued forward in no rush.

"What you did to that guy," Traise replied, "with the arm and head thing."

The old man took another pull on his cigar, removed it from his mouth, spit on the burning end to extinguish it, and placed in back in his shirt pocket. "Oh, that? Just a little something I've learned since being here."

Richard joined in from behind them. "And where is *here* exactly?" he asked as the other three behind him listened intently.

The old man stopped and turned around, halting the five in their tracks. Still holding the lantern, he stretched both arms straight out from his side and rotated his torso to the left and right while looking around him. He then lowered his arms slowly and looked at his five new guests.

"Just … here," he said. Then he smiled. "Damn, I'm thirsty," he said, turned, and resumed walking the dock.

As Traise and Richard walked side by side with Gendo, Sam, and Steve close behind, and the old man still leading, Traise said in a lowered voice, "I don't know what the hell is going on, but I've got a few questions for this Chief fella."

Without missing a beat, Richard uttered back to him, "You and me both, brother." After a slight pause, he repeated, "You and me both."

Chapter Four

It was a short, ten-minute walk from the dock up a worn dirt path gradually engulfed by thick vegetation and trees on both sides. The old man, Samuel Hartman, known as "Chief," strolled casually in front of the five as if he had not a worry in the world, the kerosene lantern at his side swinging slightly with each step. There was no further conversation during the walk as the five behind him followed in silence while intently observing their surroundings but keeping a close eye on their escort.

Before long, a small log cabin became visible in front of them, a light wisp of smoke lifting from the stone chimney at one end and a glow of yellow light emitting from two small windows in the front next to the entrance. As they approached the rustic building, the air temperature dropped dramatically. Even though it was July, it suddenly felt like a fall day with a chill in the air. Autumn-colored leaves covered the ground and became more plentiful the closer they got. It was difficult to see any details of the exterior in the moonlight, but Traise did notice two old metal bait buckets sitting side by side next to the front door and a variety of old-style fishing poles leaning against the worn wooden exterior.

Because they were dressed for summer in shorts and t-shirts, the five visitors became even more aware of the cool air. Richard turned to Traise and said, "What the hell? Feels like it just turned into November!"

Before Traise could respond, the old man chuckled and said, "My favorite time of year!" and he reached out with his right hand, grasped the black handle of the door, and pushed down the thumb lever to raise the small iron bar from the metal latch.

As Chief was about to open the door, Traise spoke out. "How did it just go from eighty degrees out here to feeling like it might snow?"

Samuel Hartman turned to him while opening the door and said with a slight grin, "When you're here, anything is possible." Then, following a slight pause, "And anything is real."

He took a few steps into the cabin, held up the kerosene lantern, raised the glass globe, and blew out the flame. "Welcome, gentlemen. Please come in and make yourselves comfortable while I get you something to drink." He walked over and disappeared through a small doorway into another room off to the left of the main room.

As the five entered, each of them felt a sudden comfortable calmness even though they were all still quite apprehensive of their situation.

The warmth from the small crackling fire slowly rid them of the brisk crispness that they had briefly walked through outside.

Sam immediately went to the fireplace and knelt down in front of the flaming warmth, reached out his hands with his palms facing the fire then began rubbing his hands together. "Feels like we're in a Rockwell painting," he said as he watched the dancing flames in front of him.

Gendo walked over and stood beside him. "I was thinking more of Hansel and Gretel myself. This is just weird," he whispered, enjoying the heat beside his friend.

Steve was now sitting silently in an old wooden rocking chair in one corner of the room, still amazed and confused, rubbing his arm and flexing it up and down and side-to-side, looking for any trace of his injury. Traise and Richard were standing in the middle of the room next to each other, looking around at their surroundings.

The entire interior of the cabin was sparse, with only a few pieces of wooden furniture. A round table with a lit lantern sitting on it was against the right wall with a chair on each side. The fireplace in front of them was made of multi-colored stone and extended from the floor all the way up to the ceiling with various iron hooks attached on each side of the fire pit with metal utensils and a small leather bag hanging from them. A large black kettle sat on a flat stone just beside the opening, and an iron tripod with the legs out and a large hook dangling down from the apex was sitting in the pit extending just above the fire. Another larger rocking chair sat on the opposite side just off to the side of the fireplace. The floor was wooden and featured a few large, oval, rag-tied rugs with one under the table, one in front of the fireplace, and another just inside the front door. There were only two small, four-pane windows with no curtains or blinds, one on each side of the entrance. Against the other wall was more fishing equipment: old reels, poles, and a couple of fly fishing rods. A small canvas bag with various lures hooked into the sides was open with even more lures visible inside.

Speaking in a low tone as he looked around, Traise said to Richard, "You notice anything strange?"

Still taking in the interior of the room, Richard responded in almost a whisper, "You mean like everything?"

Traise nodded. "Well, there's that, but look around. There's no pictures anywhere. No paper or magazines. Nothing electrical like a refrigerator, radio, television, or even a phone."

Richard looked around, but before he could answer, Chief re-appeared from the side room with a tray. On it were two bottles, two tin cups, and a small wooden cup about the size of a large shot glass.

He first walked to Traise and Richard and said, "I believe beer is the beverage of choice for you two," as he handed each of them an opened bottle. They took the drinks and looked at each other curiously.

The old man then walked over to Gendo and handed him one of the tins with steam rising from the hot beverage. "French Vanilla Latte for you, sir." Gendo took the hot cup gingerly as he looked at Traise and Richard with wide eyes.

Chief then turned to Steve. "Black with a touch of Irish Cream for you, Mr. Adams?" he said as he held out the other tin.

Steve reached out for the drink and responded in almost a stutter, "Ummm, yeah. That's perfect. Thank you."

Finally, he held out the small wooden cup to Sam. "And I believe you'll find this the smoothest Tequila that you've ever tasted, Mr. Willow."

Sam reached out slowly and took the drink with a slightly shaking hand. He looked at the host as he raised the liquor to his lips, took a sip, raised his eyebrows, smiled, and said simply, "Ahhhh."

Traise watched intently and in amazement at the delivery to each of them and, once Sam had his drink, said to Chief, "How did you know exactly what each of us liked?"

Samuel Hartman pulled the cigar again from his shirt pocket and placed it in his mouth, took out his lighter and lit the end, taking a long drag. He blew the smoke back out from his mouth and said, looking at each of them, "I could say it was a lucky guess, but that wouldn't exactly be accurate." Samuel Hartman walked over to the fireplace and took the leather bag from one of the hooks, untied the top that was cinched closed with leather strips, and pulled a glass bottle from it. With his cigar and his bottle in hand, the old man sat down in the rocking chair next to the fireplace, pulled the stopper out of the bottle, and took a long swig.

"Have a seat, gentleman," he said. "I imagine there are quite a few questions you would like answered." He took another toke on the cigar and another drink from the bottle, "But please be aware, the answers I will provide will not be easy to comprehend." Following another puff on his cigar, he smiled and said, "Now, who's first?"

* * *

Before Traise could say anything, Richard took a sip from his bottle, looked at Samuel Hartman, and said, "So where exactly are we?"

Chief took another extended puff from his cigar and leaned forward looking intently toward the five men. "You are somewhere, but you are nowhere. It is on no map, but yet has been talked about since the beginning of time. It is a place with as many occupants as there are stars in the sky, but you only see those that you choose to see." Richard stared at the old man for a second, then turned to Traise with raised eyebrows and said sarcastically, "Well, that clears things up."

Traise returned the look to Richard, then turned back to the old man and said, "Well, does this place have a name?"

The old man switched his gaze to Traise. "It has many names, depending on what you believe. Whatever you call it, it is exactly that. Some call it Nirvana, some Utopia, some Shangri-La, some Valhalla, and some ..." after a slight pause, he continued, "... some call it Heaven." He then sat back in the rocking chair and continued, "I myself prefer the term Athanasia. Has a certain ring to it," he said with a wink.

Sam, almost choking on his drink upon hearing Chief, swallowed hard, wiped his mouth, and said in astonishment, "Heaven? Did you say Heaven?"

Traise reached over to his friend and patted him on the back a few times. "Easy there, Sam. I think we stumbled upon a crazy man here," he said as he looked at their host.

Richard walked over to the wooden table and set his bottle on it, looked at the others, and said, "I think it's time for us to go, guys."

Just as he was turning towards the door, there was a quick knock, and the door opened. A young man, appearing to be in his twenties entered, dressed in worn jeans, a red flannel shirt, and a black baseball cap with a large yellow "P" on the front. "Hey Gramps!" he said as he came through the door, not noticing the cabin's occupants immediately. He stopped when he saw the others, looked at each of them, and said, "Oh, sorry. I didn't know you had visitors. I can come back later if you want."

Samuel Hartman gave a slight chuckle as he stood up from the rocking chair and approached the young man. "No, no, no. Come on in," he said as he hugged the young man. "Came across these gentlemen while out fishing. They ran into some trouble, and I brought them back here. I was just explaining to them where they're at."

The younger man hesitated briefly as he looked at the five and asked, "New arrivals?"

The old man relinquished the hug and walked back to his rocking chair. "We were just getting to that," he stated as he sat back down, "Gentleman, let me introduce my Grandson. This is Joshua Hartman."

The younger Hartman walked toward the five with his arm extended and shook each of their hands. "Pleasure to meet you," he said to each of them. "Please call me Josh. I'm sure you're a bit confused about what's going on."

Richard was the last to shake his hand and while doing so said, "That's an understatement."

Josh smiled as he released Richard's hand. "Totally understandable. I felt the same way when I arrived here. I ask that you be patient with Gramps. He has a roundabout way of explaining things."

Gendo, who had been quiet through all of the conversation, chimed in. "So when did you get here?"

Josh turned towards him and said, "1983."

Traise immediately blurted out, "Did you say 1983?"

Josh nodded his head up and down, "I did. November of 1983."

Steve stood straight up from his chair, looking at the young man, and said, "That's impossible! That would be over thirty-five years ago!"

Joshua Hartman turned his attention towards Steve and said with a half-smile, "If I was counting, that would be about right."

Richard walked over to Josh and looked him square in the eyes. "But you look like you're only in your twenties! Don't tell me you're going to give us the same lines as this guy," he said as he pointed to Chief.

Josh looked at his grandfather, tilted his head slightly, and said, "Gramps, maybe you should continue."

The old man, who had been sitting with an amused look on his face during the conversation, took a swig from his bottle and said, "Yep, guess I better. Please, have a seat and relax gentleman. I will try to explain things a little more clearly to you." He then leaned forward in his chair with his elbows on his knees and looked seriously at each of them, "You see, when you come here, you remain just as you were upon arrival."

Traise looked at Richard as the old man spoke. "Here we go again," he said to his life-long friend.

Samuel Hartman held his hand up gently as if asking Traise to let him continue. "You have arrived at a place the same as many have before you. There comes a time when every soul ceases to be as they know it and a new existence is born. This is where that new existence begins. And what an existence it is! You have what you want and live as you wish, wherever you choose. There is no need for anything, as it is provided to you. You may be as I have chosen to be, here in a small cabin in the woods free to do what I want, when I want." Then he looked with an approving smile at Josh and continued. "And to see who I want, when I want." Turning back to the five, he said, "You may choose to live in a big city surrounded by others who wish to do the same. It is completely up to you. There are no worries, no stress, no confrontations, no governments to dictate how you shall exist, no religion to cause wars because you may not believe as they do. There is no time, calendar, or year. There is no sadness, but there is excitement. No hate, but there is love. No disappointment, but there is pride. There is no pain or suffering, and hunger is non-existent. There is satisfaction to do or accomplish whatever you wish, but there are challenges."

As the five listened in astonishment to the words they were hearing, Traise suddenly shook his head from side to side and interrupted the old man. "Are you trying to tell us that we're actually in Heaven?"

Chief turned to Traise with a calming look. "Call it what you will, Mr. Robbins, but it is exactly whatever you believe. But not everything is perfect," he continued, a hint of sadness in his voice. "My son, Joshua's father David, has his own existence here. He has his own free will. Oh, we see him now and then, but he's off on his own adventures, and those adventures don't always involve us."

Josh spoke softly, "My son, too. Joshua Jr."

"We call him J.J.," the old man said with obvious pride.

Traise asked, "You have a son?"

"Yes," Josh replied. "He was born after I came here. But I've had some time to get to know him since then. Not as much time as I'd like because he likes to join my father on his adventures. I'm happy that they've bonded so well, but I miss them both when they're gone."

Richard stared unbelievingly at Chief and then at Josh and then back at the old man again. "If what you're saying is true, and I hardly believe that it is, then you're telling us that we're dead. Correct?" Then looking at the others, he said, "I don't know about you guys, but I certainly don't feel dead."

Josh, now standing beside his grandfather with a hand on the old man's shoulder, smiled and said, "We don't like to use the word 'dead' here. Seems so final. We prefer the term 'the next step.'"

Samuel Hartman reached up and patted his grandson's hand as he continued. "I realize what I have said is almost impossible for you to comprehend, but let me ask you something," he said as he pointed around the cabin. "The fire in front of you has been burning the same as when you walked in, and yet you see no wood around it. The season changed as you walked closer to this cabin although it is your summer. The drinks that you're enjoying remain full even though you have been consuming them. And you were witness to Mr. Adams's sudden recovery from his injuries. How could this be if I'm not speaking the truth?"

At these words, all four of the friends and Steve instantly looked at their individual drinks and saw that all had somehow been replenished. They immediately looked at each other in astonishment, and Sam began to shake as he said with a quivering voice to the old man, "Are you God?"

Chief and Josh each let out a burst of laughter with the old man quipping, "Oh my, no! I don't want that responsibility!" As his laughter subsided he continued. "Let's just say I'm a host that enjoys greeting those who come here and tries to make their transition a bit more comfortable."

As they all sat in stone-faced silence, trying to understand but not completely accepting the situation, Traise noticed that Josh had gone into the side room for an instant and returned with a small piece of paper in his hand that he then tucked into his jeans pocket. He then went back and stood beside his grandfather without saying a word.

Richard, still in a somewhat shocked state, looked at Chief and said, "What about our families and friends back home? What about them? Can't we say goodbye?"

The old man again smiled, "When you arrive here, it's not the end of you to them. You can visit or communicate with anyone you wish at any time. Just not the way you're accustomed to."

Richard looked at him with a quizzical look and said, "What do you mean by that?"

Chief leaned back in his chair and took a drink from his bottle. "Did you ever have a dream of a friend or someone you loved that has, what you would call, died?"

Richard looked at Traise and the others and said, "I think we all have. So?"

The old man continued, "And they always look the same as you remember them?"

Gendo jumped into the conversation saying, "Because they remain the same as when they arrived?"

The old man nodded in the affirmative and said, "Because there is no time here. And, have you ever lost something that you know where it should be because that's the last place you put it,

79

but you find it somewhere else that it shouldn't be? Or a wooden spoon, utensil, or something of that nature all of a sudden is missing from the drawer it's always in, and then later it's back in the drawer?"

All five of the guests looked at each other and nodded up and down, knowing exactly what was described. The old man chuckled, saying, "We still have a sense of humor. We're just letting you know that we're still around. We can't be serious all the time, ya know. We miss our loved ones just as you do, and sometimes we want to let you know that we're still around. It may be a simple gesture such as a butterfly landing on your hand or a cardinal appearing outside your window looking in or even a leaf falling from a tree and gently landing on your shoulder. All of these, and more, are some ways that we communicate."

The room was completely silent as the five sat motionless, each contemplating and trying to absorb the information that was just presented to them. Confusion, disbelief, and sadness were evident on each of their faces, as their fate had been exposed.

With his head lowered, a single tear formed in the corner of Traise's eye, slowly running down his cheek before dropping to the wooden floor. He lifted his head to look at the old man and said, "So what happens now?"

Chief smiled, took yet another swig from his bottle, and reinserted the cork stopper into the top of it. "Right now, my grandson and I will take you back to your boat."

As if synchronized, the other four sharply lifted their heads with Richard saying, "Back to the boat? Why are we going back to the boat?"

Samuel Hartman lifted himself from his chair and walked over to the fireplace, reaching for the black leather bag, and placing the bottle back inside. He then pulled the leather tie, cinching it closed, and hung the bag on the hook. Then he turned back to them and said, "Because you're going home. It's not your time to be here."

Chapter Five

The shock of the old man's words reverberated through each of them. "We're going home?" said Sam loudly.

Chief nodded. "Yes, Mr. Willow. You are going home."

With this new revelation, Traise shook his head from side to side from confusion and said, "I don't understand. You just told us all about this place and what happens when we arrive. Now you say we're going home?"

The old man walked to the door and picked up his lantern. "That is correct, Mr. Robbins. Although it appears so here, as I said, perfection is unattainable. You and your friends happened to be in the wrong place at the wrong time. It was never intended that you become involved in the fate of Mr. Adams."

Steve's head jerked toward the old man, and he blurted out, "Wait, what do you mean, *my fate?*"

The old man turned his body to face Steve and said in a calm manner, "When your plane crashed, Mr. Adams, it was meant to be because it was your time. These four gentlemen and their vessel were not supposed to be at that location to witness the event and, as commendable as it was, certainly were not supposed to risk their lives to rescue you. You were, in fact, destined to take the next step in your existence, which was to come here."

Steve stared at the old man in stunned disbelief and stuttered, "But I want to go back home with them. I don't want to stay here!"

Richard spoke up, saying, "We can't leave him here. He's going with us!"

Chief shifted his position to address Richard. "There is no option, Mr. Drewer. This is Mr. Adams's time." After a slight pause, he turned back to Steve. "Actually, Mr. Adams, there is a choice that I can offer you, but you must decide right now."

Steve's eyes widened with sudden excitement. "What is it? What choice? Please tell me!"

Chief remained calm and said with a firmness that had not been present before, "Your choice is that you may remain here and continue what was meant to be, or you may return to the boat with these four. However, you must know and absolutely understand that if you choose to board the vessel, upon your arrival at the location of the incident, your existence will cease completely. You will not return home, and you will not take the next step."

Traise walked over and stood side by side with Richard as the old man continued.

"You will simply vanish from their presence, and it will be the final of finals with no reprieve." He then turned and looked at the other four individually. "Mr. Robbins, Mr. Drewer, Mr. Gendo, and Mr. Willow, you have experienced what very few have been able to experience. You have seen what shall be when you take the next step. But unlike the many before you, you are returning to your lives as you know them. Take what you have seen, felt, and thought while here with you so you can remember what lies ahead when your time comes. When that does occur, do not fear it, as you now know what awaits. You will return and be welcomed with open arms."

Chief turned back to Steve. "Mr. Adams, your decision?"

Steve, with his eyes welling up, looked at the old man. "This has to be a dream, doesn't it? I must have passed out in the crash, and this is just a dream. I've worked hard in my law practice for decades. I was going to retire soon and spend more time flying, more time just for myself. I just need to wake up and everything will be okay, right?"

Chief moved closer to Steve, placed a hand on each of his shoulders, and squeezed gently. "It is no dream, Mr. Adams, and I have no benefit from whichever you choose. I was granted the same choice as you a long time ago, so I understand the conflict within. What I am able to tell you is that I made the correct decision just as I know you will as well."

Steve looked into the eyes of the old man for a few seconds, took a step back, and turned to the other four as well as Josh Hartman. He looked at each of them as silence surrounded the group. His head slowly tilted downward, and his shoulders slumped slightly. He took a deep breath and exhaled slowly as he lifted his head and nodded slightly at the old man. He then walked over to the rocker at the side of the fireplace, turned it so it faced the flickering flames, and gently lowered himself into the chair. With his elbows on each of the chair arms, he grasped his hands together, rested his chin on them, and stared into the fire.

"The decision has been made," said the old man as they all watched Steve take his seat and accept his fate. "Now, if you gentlemen will follow, Joshua and I will return you to the dock." He picked up the lantern that he had placed on the floor earlier, raised the globe, and took a match from his pocket, rubbing it sharply up his shorts, causing the small flame to erupt. Then he relit the wick inside.

The four friends stood together, alternating looks at each other and to Steve. After a second,

Traise looked at Richard and said in an exhausted tone, "I guess we should be going."

Richard, still looking at Steve sitting in the rocking chair, said in a voice barely audible, "Yeah, guess so."

Chief opened the door and stood to the side with the lantern held out in front of him towards the outside. "This way gentleman."

The four slowly turned to exit the cabin, one after the other with Sam being the last to walk past the old man. He stopped, turned around, and again looked at Steve sitting in front of the fire. He then looked at the old man saying in a hushed voice, "Is he going to be okay?"

The old man gave a single nod to Sam and said with a smile, "Mr. Adams will be just fine." Sam turned back to Steve and said aloud, "Goodbye Mr. Adams." Steve didn't move or acknowledge the words as Sam turned and followed the others. Chief stepped out and Josh Hartman exited last, pulling the wooden door closed behind him.

The trip back to the dock was just as the walk earlier to the cabin, albeit with one less member of the group. The old man and his lantern had taken the lead with Traise, Richard, Gendo, and Sam silently following closely. Josh Hartman was behind Sam as they all made their way back down the path. The air temperature had started to increase as they left the cabin further behind. The autumn colored leaves became sparse with each step, and the greenness and feel of summer returned.

*　*　*

With the old man continuing to lead, the dock slowly became visible through the now plentiful foliage. After just a few more steps, they arrived at the first boards of the wooden pier where they had moored the boat a few hours earlier. As the six of them made their way towards the tied up vessel, Richard turned his head towards Traise and, in a low voice with a hint of surprise said, "Look at the boat."

Traise gazed at the Grady White and immediately noticed that the antennas that had been ripped from the top of the boat by Steve Adams's plane were again mounted in position on the top of the cabin as if they had never been damaged. "What the hell?" Traise whispered as they continued down the pier.

Chief chuckled and, without turning his head, said just loud enough to be heard, "We really try not to use that word, Mr. Robbins."

With each advancing step, the boat's appearance became more evident to them. The almost twenty-year-old vessel glimmered as the moonlight reflected off her now pristine paint. The wear and tear of her life on the water was nowhere to be seen. The stainless steel of the rails, davits, and trim sparkled as if brand new. The cushions looked like they had never been sat on, and the deck appeared almost sterile.

The old man stopped on the dock as he reached the boat, turned to those behind him, and extended his arm as if showing a prize on a game show. "Your chariot awaits, gentlemen. I believe you will find everything in order."

Richard slowly walked from the bow to the stern, inspecting the boat from top to bottom in amazement. "It looks like it just came off the showroom floor!" he exclaimed to the others as they all gathered together and looked upon what floated before them.

Chief had a huge grin on his face as he stated, "Thank you, Mr. Drewer. We do what we can. Now, if you would, it's time for your departure."

Richard stepped onto the boat first and immediately proceeded to the controls, looking at them as if it was the first time he was on board.

As the others began to follow, the old man continued. "You will find your fuel tanks are full, and all your electronics will function normally once you break through."

Richard turned from the console of the boat towards the old man. "What do you mean, 'break through'?"

The old man gave a single nod to him and, with a half a smile, said calmly, "You will know it when it happens, Mr. Drewer."

As Richard and the Chief conversed, and before he stepped onto the boat, Traise felt a light tap on his shoulder and turned around to face the younger Hartman. Josh peered into Traise's eyes as they stood face-to-face. Josh reached into his pocket and pulled out the same slip of paper that Traise has noticed earlier in the cabin.

"Please, Mr. Robbins," he said softly. "When you return, I would be forever grateful if you would do this for me." And he transferred the note into Traise's hand. Traise looked down and unfolded the small piece of paper. On it were just a few words. "Annie Hartman, Hyndman, Pa."

Traise looked back up at Josh in an inquisitive manner but didn't say anything. As he remained locked into Traise's eyes, Josh continued, "Tell her it's okay. She'll know what you mean."

Not looking away, Traise put the paper into his pocket, shook the young man's hand, and said just as softly, "You have my word."

Josh released the handshake, smiled, and said, "Thank you, Mr. Robbins." He then turned and walked toward the rear of the boat, "I'll take the stern line, Gramps, if you'll handle the bow line."

Traise stepped onto the boat and joined Sam and Gendo as they stood beside Richard at the console. Richard turned the key in the ignition, and the twin Yamaha engines sprang to life immediately with an excited rumble. Chief and Josh had untied the bow and stern lines, tossed them onto the boat, and stood side-by-side as Richard engaged the engines to pull away from the dock.

Before he guided the vessel outward from them, Richard yelled out to the old man, "Hey, Chief! Since I don't have any navigation yet, which way do we head?"

The old man held out his arm and pointed into the dark, star-filled sky toward the brightly lit orb that was now only a third above the horizon. "Follow the moon, Mr. Drewer. Follow the moon."

Richard gave a slight salute to the old man in acknowledgment and began to turn the boat slowly away from the dock. He looked at the other three and placed his hand back on the throttle. "Let's go home, boys," he said as he pushed the lever forward, and the two V250 engines roared as the propellers bit into the water.

During the quick acceleration, the four friends turned and looked back to wave goodbye to their mysterious hosts. On the dock, Samuel Hartman stood with the lantern still in his hand. He and his grandson waved back, and then they turned together and began walking back along the pier toward land.

With the engines now at full throttle, Richard raised his eyes to the sky and altered his heading directly toward the moon as instructed by the old man. The reflection of the declining moon on the water appeared to provide a "road" for him to follow, guiding them toward whatever was waiting for them.

Without looking at the other three, he said loud enough to be heard over the engines and wind, "Follow the moon? That's some unique directions right there."

Traise leaned in toward Richard and asked, "Any idea what he meant when he said we would get instruments back when we 'broke through'?"

Richard shook his head as he continued to look over the bow while navigating. "Not a clue. I guess we'll find out soon enough." He turned to Sam and Gendo and nodded towards the door to the living space below. "You guys can go below if you want. Traise and I will stay up here. We'll get you if anything happens."

The two looked at each other, shrugged their shoulders, gave a thumbs-up to Richard, and disappeared into the compartment. Richard held a steady hand on the wheel as he said loudly to Traise, "Keep an eye out for anything that looks unusual."

Traise peered out to the sea before them and asked sarcastically, "You mean like a storm or a plane?"

Richard raised his eyebrows at his friend, feigning disgust. "Good Lord, let's hope not." The thirty-foot vessel and its passengers, two below deck and two above, remained on course, not veering from the directions given by Samuel Hartman. For twenty minutes, with the moon directly in front of them, their path continued without incident, the boat cutting through the smooth water almost effortlessly, carrying them all to whatever awaited.

* * *

Below deck, and with exhaustion overtaking them, Sam and Gendo had quickly fallen asleep. The smooth sound of the engines running and the minor rocking of the boat from side to side had them both out within what seemed to be seconds. Suddenly, the sound of the engines cutting back woke them up simultaneously. Each sat straight up and looked at the other with mild excitement.

"You think we're back?" Sam said, staring at Gendo.

"The way this trip has gone, I wouldn't bet the farm on it," Gendo said as he cleared his head from sleep. "Let's go see what's going on." He grabbed and turned the handle on the compartment door and took the short two steps up and out onto the deck with Sam right behind him.

Richard was still at the controls and Traise was off to the starboard side, both looking intently forward beyond the bow of the boat. Gendo stood beside Richard and asked, "What's happening?"

Richard continued looking ahead while pulling back more on the throttle control until the boat was barely moving. With his other arm and hand, he pointed out over the bow and said with a hint of concern, "That's what's happening."

Sam and Gendo each looked out and saw what had Richard and Traise's attention. Directly ahead of them was a wide area of extreme darkness that stretched out for miles on both sides. No stars or horizon was visible anywhere within the area.

"What the hell is that?" Sam asked while holding on to the side of the enclosure that surrounded the helm area.

"Your guess is as good as mine, Sam. I'm hoping it's just a fog bank," Traise chimed in. "We came upon it pretty fast. It's like it's just sitting there."

Gendo broke his gaze, turned to Richard, and said with apprehension, "Don't tell me it's another storm."

Richard scanned the area directly in front of them and said with a sense of confidence, "I don't think so. I don't see any lightning, the wind is still calm, and the waves aren't picking up at all."

Traise returned to his friend's side at the helm and again looked out into the area of blackness. "You think that's what the old man was talking about?"

Richard shrugged his shoulders. "Could be." Pausing for a second, he continued, "There's only one way to find out." With a sudden spark of determination, Richard looked at the other three and said calmly, "Hold on, boys. Here we go."

With his left hand, he tightened his grip on the wheel, firmly wrapped the fingers of his right hand around the lever of the throttle control, and pushed it hard forward. As the engines kicked in and the propellers again took hold, the bow jumped upward out of the water. The power of the engines quickly had the boat on a level plane with the keel barely in the water, hurtling them at full speed toward the blackness that lay ahead.

* * *

The change was instant and dramatic as they entered into the abyss. With the exception of the vessel's red and green running lights, their entire surroundings were void of any other light. There was no visible horizon line as the sky and the sea appeared to morph into one. The sea remained glass-like with no swells or waves and only the sound of the engines and the wind blowing against them creating any noise. They remained together on deck, shoulder to shoulder, surrounding Richard as he maintained his tight grip on the wheel and the throttle at full power. All were transfixed, straining to see anything before them, but only complete blackness was visible.

The tension was high and palpable. All four friends were filled with a mix of apprehension, anxiety, and fear as the vessel continued at full speed through the nothingness. Each man remained stoic as they continued to focus ahead. They had been in the black hole-like area for only ten minutes, but it seemed like an eternity. Without warning, the radio began to crackle with static, and the lights on the control panel flickered dimly. All four immediately looked at the panel and then at each other.

Sam blurted out, "What does that mean?"

Without breaking his concentration, Richard said loudly, "I know what I hope it means."

As soon as the last word exited his mouth, and in a blink of an eye, it was as if they had burst through some invisible barrier. The blackness instantly disappeared. In an instant, stars were visible in the night sky as moonlit brightness engulfed them. Richard pulled back on the throttle control, slowing the boat instantly as the bow sunk down into the water.

Traise turned his head toward the stern and was amazed at what he saw, or rather, what he didn't see. "It's gone!" he said loudly.

The other three together turned toward the back of the boat and saw nothing but the sea and clear sky. As they all gazed around them, not one of them noticed that the control panel lights were now fully lit. The compass was no longer erratic but had settled into a steady indication that they were heading dead west. The GPS had reacquired its signal, and their exact location was now displayed on the small monitor that showed the outline of a land mass directly in front of them. As they turned back, each pointed outward over the bow. In the distance, lights were now visible, and the slow rotating light beam from the Assateague Lighthouse shown out in all directions.

With a slight grin, Richard turned to Traise. "I think we just broke through."

Traise nodded to his friend and, with a sigh of relief, said, "I do believe you're correct. How far out are we?"

Richard looked at the GPS as he inched the throttle forward, increasing power to the engines. "Looks like about two miles from the harbor entrance. Should be there in about ten minutes."

With that news, Sam and Gendo broke into smiles and high-fived each other with instant enthusiasm. Traise slapped his friend on the back saying, "Take us in, Captain Dick."

Richard pushed the throttle completely forward, turned to Traise, and said, "You got it, brother. Let's go home."

* * *

The first signs of daylight were appearing as Richard pulled back the throttle and turned the boat into Curtis Merritt Harbor. They could see the activity of a few vehicles making their way with boats in tow toward the launch ramp, undoubtedly readying for a leisurely day on the water either fishing, crabbing, or just enjoying the beautiful day that was about to be.

Richard spotted an open slip close to the ramp and guided the vessel bow into the opening. Without being asked, Traise stepped up on the bow with bow line in hand and, when the boat was only a foot or so away, he hopped up on the dock and looped the line over the wooden piling, keeping the line slack as Richard backed down and turned the wheel, bringing the stern in towards the dock. Traise tightened and secured the bow line and made his way towards the rear of the boat where Gendo was waiting to toss him the stern line. They moved like a crew now, not separate individuals.

After receiving and securing the line, Traise sat down with his legs dangling off the dock, crossed his arms on his chest, leaned back, and let out an audible sigh.

Sam wasted no time in getting off the boat, jumping onto the dock, falling to his knees, leaning forward, and kissing the wooden structure. "Terra Firma, oh how I love thee!" he said as he rolled over onto his back and looked at Traise. "Is Chatties open this early?" Sam asked.

Traise turned his head toward his friend. "Not for a couple of hours," he said with a grin.

Sam looked at him with disappointment. "That's quite unfortunate. I could really go for one of those Laura Crushes you guys have been talking about."

With the boat secured to dock, Richard placed the throttle in neutral and turned the ignition key to the left, silencing the engines. "I'll head over to the Harbor Master office and see if Vernon will let us stayed tied up here for a couple hours. We'll come back later, put this thing on the trailer, and pull her out." He then turned to Gendo, who was sitting down at the stern with his head down, "You ready to go ashore?"

Gendo glanced up with an exhausted look on his face, nodded his head slowly up and down, and, with eyebrows raised, said, "Ready to go ashore and sure as hell ready to stay ashore."

Richard smiled and responded to all three men, "I think we all are, at least for a while. You guys gather up your things and head to the truck while I go see Vernon." He then stepped onto the dock and headed towards the office. Gendo stood up as Traise and Sam slowly raised themselves off the dock and returned to the boat to begin collecting their belongings in silence.

* * *

Half an hour later, Richard exited the office of the Harbor Master and walked toward the lot where the truck was parked and peered through the opened window on the driver's side. Traise was in the passenger seat, and Sam and Gendo were sitting in the rear. All three sat with their eyes closed, exhausted from the events that they had just been through.

"Hey Traise," Richard said in his captain's voice, "grab the cooler from the back. We forgot to get the fish out of the bin. Don't want them to go bad."

Traise turned his head and with only one eye open said, "Really?"

Richard gave him a slightly serious look and responded, "Come on. It will only take a minute. We have to get them on ice, and then we can get back to the house and get some sleep. Vernon said we can stay moored up until noon, and then we have to get the boat out."

With a feigned heavy sigh, Traise opened the passenger side door and walked to the back of the truck. He pulled the large cooler from the bed and joined his friend as they made their way back to the dock. As Traise and Richard headed to the boat to retrieve the catch, Gendo, still with his eyes closed and not moving a muscle, mumbled to Sam, "I never liked fish."

Richard stepped down onto the boat and turned back as Traise handed the cooler down to him. Richard grabbed the large container by the side handles and took a few steps to the stern where the fish bin was located. Then he placed the cooler on the deck and unlocked the hatch to the bin. Opening the lid, he stood straight up and turned to Traise, who had just stepped down onto the boat.

"Holy shit," Richard said. "Come look at this!"

Traise joined him, and they both stared at the contents in front of them.

"Looks like Chief had one more surprise for us," Traise said as he looked down into the bin. Inside were not just the ten or twelve fish that they had caught previously. At least three times as many filled the hold with a multitude of Rockfish, Flounder, Grouper, Mahi-mahi, and a few others that they didn't recognize calmly maneuvering around each other in the water-filled storage container.

The men quickly began to extract the catch, placing each lively fish in the cooler as Richard said calmly, "I hope that's the last surprise he has for us."

Without hesitation, Traise reciprocated to his friend, "Got that right." He looked at the cooler and at the remaining fish in the bin. Then he stood straight up and looked at Richard, saying in a deadpan voice, "I think we're gonna need a bigger cooler."

* * *

It was quite unusual for the four friends to be so quiet for so long when together. After leaving the harbor, they drove to the rental house, unloaded their gear, put the fish on ice, and retreated to their individual bedrooms. With the exception of short banter, they didn't speak, and they certainly didn't talk about anything relating to their recent experience on the boat.

Traise and Richard opted to take showers while Sam and Gendo collapsed on their beds, asleep as soon as their heads hit the pillows. It didn't take long for Traise and Richard to follow closely behind as all four were completely exhausted from the events of the last twenty-four hours or so. After a too-short few hours of sleep, Richard and Traise returned to the harbor to trailer the boat, leaving Sam and Gendo at the house to get a bit more rest. Upon returning, they woke their friends, who then showered and changed clothes, and the four men headed back out for a mid-morning meal at Chatties Lounge, the bar and extended eatery located upstairs above Don's Seafood Restaurant on Main Street in downtown Chincoteague.

As Richard pulled the truck into the parking lot, Sam noticed how full it was with cars in just about every available space. "Pretty busy for a Sunday morning isn't it?" he said as Richard slowly toured the lot searching for a parking space.

"It's always like this on Sundays," Traise said from the front seat. "It's chicken and dumplings every Sunday morning here. All the church people come in after services. It'll clear out in a bit. Besides, we're going upstairs, and it's not as busy up there."

After finding an open spot in the rear of the parking lot, they exited the truck and walked back toward the restaurant and up the side steps to the Chatties entrance. Inside were a couple people sitting around the bar and a few more at the individual tables by the windows that overlooked Main Street. Behind the bar was an attractive, spunky woman who looked to be in her thirties with a slim build and a short, black, slightly spiked haircut, and stylish black-rimmed eyeglasses.

"Hey, Traise! Hey, Richard! Haven't seen y'all in a while. Have a seat anywhere and I'll be right with ya," she said with her southern draw and a bright, cheerful smile.

Traise turned to Sam and Gendo, saying quietly, "That would be Laura."

Sam smiled and responded, "You mean of 'Laura Crush' fame?"

Richard nodded, adding, "That would be the one."

They took their seats at one of the window tables, and Laura chirped up from behind the bar while mixing a drink for another customer, "Can I get y'all something to drink?"

Sam immediately raised his hand and said, "Yes Ma'am. One Laura Crush here!"

Traise, Richard, and Gendo all followed with, "Same here!"

Laura flashed her smile and said, "You got it! Y'all need menus too?"

In unison, all four said, "Yes, please."

As they waited for their drinks and menus, Traise broke the ice saying, "So … what do we make of our little …" he held his fingers up in air quotes "… fishing trip?"

Gendo leaned forward, speaking softly. "If I hadn't been there, I never would have believed it." After a slight pause, he continued. "I'm really not sure I do believe it."

Richard, also leaning forward and speaking in a low volume, said, "Nobody's gonna believe it. I think this is something we all agree will be kept between us and no one else."

Sam entered the conversation, looking at the others and saying, "Do you really think that we were where the old man said we were?"

Traise shook his head from side to side slightly. "I have no idea. The whole thing was so incredible. The storm, the plane crash, the old man, and his explanations, not to mention the repairs to the boat and that black void, whatever it was, thing we went through. Like you said, Gendo, if we weren't there, it would be impossible to believe."

Sam's eyebrows raised at the mention of the plane crash, and in a hushed voice said, "Yeah, the plane crash! What do we tell people about the plane and Steve Adams?"

Richard looked sternly at Sam and then to Traise and Gendo, keeping his voice low. "We tell nobody about anything. Nobody knows that we were even there when the plane crashed, and they don't know that we know anything about Adams. As far as the rest of the world knows, we went out and had a very non-eventful fishing trip. Agreed?"

The three others looked at each other, nodded their heads in acknowledgment, and at the same time and, with low voices, said, "Agreed."

At that moment, Laura arrived at the table with menus under one arm and a tray with four large glasses filled to the rim, each with a straw and orange slice on the lip. "Here ya go, four Laura Crushes. I'll give y'all a minute to look over the menu, and I'll be back when you're ready."

Sam was the first to sample the drink, taking a large sip from his straw and then smiling. "Wow, that's good! What's in it?"

Traise took a sip from his glass, then took the orange slice from the lip and placed it into the drink, pushing it down and stirring the drink with his straw, "Freshly squeezed orange juice and vodka is all I know for sure. She puts something else in there, but she won't tell anyone what it is."

Gendo followed suit, taking a long pull on his straw and then saying, "Is it just me, or are there a lot of secrets around here."

Richard gave a slight chuckle as he looked at a menu. "There are secrets everywhere, but what isn't a secret is how frickin' hungry I am!"

After ordering, it didn't take long for Laura to deliver their food, and it took even less time for them to devour it, all the while continuing to discuss the incredible happenings, remembering and reexamining almost every last detail. At their request, Laura brought one more round of crushes and the ticket to the table.

As she began picking up the empty plates from the table, Laura looked at Traise and

Richard and said, "So what brings you back to the island? Seems like forever since I've seen you two."

The two men looked at each other and then to her, with Richard saying, "Just a weekend getaway. Brought the boat up and did a little fishing."

Laura picked up the last plate and said, "Well, you need to come back more often. It's been great to see y'all, and a pleasure to meet you two as well," she said with a smile for Sam and Gendo.

Sam lifted his glass towards her, "I am now a fan of Laura Crushes! I know I'll be back, thank you." As she turned and walked away with her arms full of plates, napkins, and silverware, Sam continued, almost in a whisper, "I'll be back, but I guarantee there won't be any boats involved."

"Well, so now what?" Gendo asked as they each sipped their crushes.

Richard took a large swig and put the glass on the table. "Back to the house. I've got a ton of fish to clean."

Sam took another sip of his drink and said, "There's a lonesome half-empty bottle of Tequila at the house that requires my immediate attention."

Gendo looked at the window and uttered, "I've had about enough excitement for the weekend. My plan is to watch the tube tonight. Maybe we can hit the beach tomorrow."

They all turned their attention to Traise as he fidgeted with his glass.

"So what about you, Traise?" Richard said to his buddy.

Traise took a sip from his drink, placed the glass on the table, and looked at his three friends. "Gonna help Richard with the fish and then get a good night's sleep. Leaving early in the morning."

The other three looked at him confused. Richard asked, "Whatcha mean, you're leaving in the morning? I thought we were all leaving on Wednesday?"

Traise looked stoically at the others. "Change of plans," he said. "There's something I've got to do."

Chapter Six

Monday was Annie's favorite day of the week because Darcy's Place restaurant was closed, which gave her a chance to enjoy a full day without having to work. She slept in a bit longer than usual this morning and didn't wake up until little Hannah started pawing at her. That was her way of letting Annie know that it was time to get up and let her outside. She glanced at the clock on the bedside table and saw that it was nine-thirty.

"Gotta go potty?" she said as she affectionately rubbed her small companion's head. Hannah immediately jumped down from the bed and scampered toward the bedroom door, stopping and turning to see if Annie was following. As soon as she saw Annie throw back the covers and place a foot on the floor, the terrier turned again and took off toward the door that led to the fenced-in back yard. Annie donned her robe, made her way through the kitchen, and turned the lock to unlatch the deadbolt on the door. Hannah waited with her tail wagging excitedly, and when Annie pushed open the wooden screened door, the little dog scurried out into the yard. Annie pulled the exterior door closed but kept the interior door open to let in some of the warm but comfortable morning air flow.

Then she turned to the kitchen counter and hit the start button on the coffee maker that she always set up the night before. She grabbed a clean cup from the cabinet and a spoon from the utensil drawer, and she placed them next to the coffee maker that was now gurgling and dripping fresh coffee into the carafe. She then retrieved the French Vanilla creamer from the refrigerator and set it next to the cup and spoon and then patiently waited until there was just enough coffee in the glass container to fill her cup. Once filled, she added the creamer, stirred it a bit, placed the spoon on the counter, and walked back to look out the screen door.

The morning was fresh with the sun shining brilliantly into the yard. "Looks like a perfect day," she said out loud as she watched Hannah chase a squirrel around the back yard. Fortunately for the squirrel, Hannah was just a step slower than it was, and the small, grey critter scampered up a tree to escape. Hannah stared up the tree at her potential prey, realized that another had gotten away, turned back with indifference, and continued sniffing around the yard.

Annie chuckled at her little friend as she exited through the screened door and took a seat in one of the patio chairs on the small deck that Bo had built for her last year. This was a perfectly relaxing start to a normal day in the small quaint town of Hyndman. She had plenty of time to shower and clean up around the house before Bo would stop by to pick her up at around one o'clock. They had made plans to do some shopping just across the state line in Cumberland, Maryland, about a twenty-minute drive from her house, and then they would grab a leisurely, late-afternoon bite to eat afterward.

As she sat sipping her coffee, watching Hannah play in the yard, and looking forward to the day, there was no way she could know that shortly, she would meet someone who would change her life forever.

* * *

Traise Robbins had hit the road at sunrise and was now driving on Interstate 70 just a few miles west of Baltimore. The night before, he looked on the internet to find where Hyndman, Pennsylvania, was, and found that it was going to be about a four-and-a-half to five-hour drive from Chincoteague. After another search, he was able to find one person by the name of Annie Hartman who had an address on Shellsburg Street in Hyndman. He figured this had to be the person on the slip of paper that was given to him on the dock by Josh Hartman. At least, he certainly hoped so. If he confirmed that this was indeed the Annie he was looking for, how in the world was he going to explain to her the reason for his visit, totally out of the blue and with a tale that nobody in his or her right mind would believe? Did she even still live in Hyndman? Would she think he was some kind of weirdo or psycho? These were just a few of the many questions running through his mind as he continued driving, exiting the interstate onto I-68 toward Cumberland, Maryland.

Traise had said goodbye to his friends earlier, waking each to let them know he was leaving and that he would be talking to them soon to explain why he had to leave earlier than planned. Although pressed by each of them, he wouldn't reveal his destination or purpose, only asking that they trust him and reassuring them that nothing was wrong. With the causeway leading to the tiny picturesque island of Chincoteague in his rearview mirror and the sun beginning to break over the horizon, he began his trek to fulfill his promise, his only clue a small piece of paper with a name and town on it in his pocket.

He took the exit from I-68 for Baltimore Street in Cumberland and continued following the directions on his phone until he saw the sign and turned onto Route 96 to Hyndman. In just a few minutes, he had crossed the Mason-Dixon Line into Pennsylvania. The landscape was entirely different from what he was used to as this was a small, two-lane road that snaked its way through the small hills in the southwest portion of the state. A country road to say the least. He was used to the flat, hardly any curves, metro area of Northern Virginia, so, as he continued, he was extremely cautious, driving under the speed limit of fifty miles per hour that was marked periodically along the way.

He encountered very little traffic to speak of, so he was able to casually observe rural America with its rolling hills, country streams, old wooden barns, and pastures featuring cows and a few goats lazily mingling together. With few exceptions, just about every house appeared to be built decades ago, showing wear and tear but reflecting and representing the hard-working people who lived in them.

After fifteen minutes or so of driving, he entered the small town of Hyndman and stopped temporarily at the only stoplight within miles, a blinking red light at the three-way intersection of Center and Shellsburg Streets, and continued straight through, now looking for the house number that he found on the internet.

Within a quarter of a mile, he saw the number he was looking for on the left side of the street and pulled over to the curb in front of the residence. It was a small house that appeared to be well maintained, with white wooden siding and dark green shutters on the sides of each window. A cement walkway led from the street to three steps and an open porch with a white-painted railing and wooden spindles the entire width of the front of the house. A two-person wooden swing hung motionless at one end, and on the other were two darkly stained rocking chairs with a small table between them. Multiple blooming flowers in small gray planters had been placed neatly within the confines of the porch, adding an inviting splash of color to the curbside appeal of the cottage-like house.

There was a single-car garage off to the left of the house with the door closed, not allowing Traise to tell if anyone was home or not. He put his car into park, turned off the ignition, and then reached into his pocket to pull out the folded piece of paper that led him to this small house in this small town. Nervously, he unfolded the note and again looked at the address he had written down. Then he checked the black numbers above the porch, verifying that this was, in fact, the address he was looking for. He took a few seconds, folded the note back up, returned it to his pocket, took a deep breath, and opened the car door. He paused for an instant, anxiously looking at the closed front door, and then began the short walk up to the porch.

Standing at the front door, he took another deep breath, said to himself, "Well, here goes nothing," and knocked four times.

* * *

Annie had finished her morning shower, dressed, and was cutting up a few small pieces of leftover chicken to add to Hannah's bowl of kibble as her hair dried when she heard the knock on the front door. She glanced at the time display on the oven and saw that it was just past eleven. Then looked down at Hannah, who was waiting patiently by her feet for her breakfast.

"That can't be Bo this early," she said to her little friend as she bent down and placed the bowl on the floor. Hannah paid no attention because the dog was only interested in the bowl and its contents. She delved into the chicken and kibble as soon as Annie set it in front of her.

Annie walked through the living room, turned the knob, and opened the door. Standing in front of her was a young man who appeared to be in his early thirties, clean cut with short, wavy red hair, wearing jeans, tennis shoes and a soccer jersey style white shirt. Through the screened door, Annie looked at the young man before her and immediately noticed that he appeared quite nervous.

"Hi," she said with a light smile on her face. "Can I help you?"

Traise looked at the attractive women who seemed to be in her fifties and gave a slight grin as he acknowledged her welcome.

"Yes Ma'am," he said. "Good morning. I'm sorry to disturb you, but I'm looking for Annie Hartman?"

Annie continued looking at the visitor. "I'm Annie Hartman," she said with an inquisitive look on her face.

Just for an instant, Traise was taken aback as he was expecting a much younger woman closer to the age of Josh Hartman, a man who looked to be in his twenties. In a split second, he remembered what the old man had told him and his friends: "You remain as you arrive." Traise surmised that this could be the Annie that he was in search of. He snapped out of his confusion and said with a brief stutter, "Um … Mrs. Hartman, my name is Traise Robbins, and I know this is going to seem pretty strange, but I was asked to find you and give you a message."

Annie tilted her head slightly. "First of all, please call me Annie. And second, a message from who?"

Traise hesitated as he looked at her, knowing what he was about to say and not knowing what kind of reaction he was going to get. He took a deep breath, and with apprehension, looked her in the eyes and said, "It's a message from Josh … Josh Hartman."

In a heartbeat, he saw the friendly look on her face turn to a mix of shock, anger, and hurt. She was stunned at the sound of her husband's name. Nobody other than Annie herself had said his name aloud in a very long time, and hearing it sent a shudder through her entire body. She stood rigid and stared at Traise, not understanding what was happening and trying to comprehend what she had just heard. Then her body began to shake slightly as she continued to look at him.

She took a step back from the door. "I don't know who you are or where you came from, but I think you should leave." She stepped to the side, reached for the doorknob, and started to slam the door shut on the stranger.

Traise raised his hand and placed it on the door just as it was about to close and blurted out, "He asked me to tell you, 'It's okay'!"

Suddenly, the door stopped, was still for a second, and then slowly opened back up. Annie peeked around the door with a look of confusion and disbelief, "What did you say?" she asked the stranger.

Traise lowered his hand slowly and looked stoically at her. "He wants you to know that it's okay."

The door opened wide again and Annie stood face to face with him, looking him directly in the eyes. "That's impossible. My husband died more than thirty years ago. What in the world possessed you to come here and say something like that to me?"

Traise could see the emotions building in her and searched for something to say that would somehow make sense but knew deep down that anything he said would only escalate the situation. "Mrs. Hartman, I know how this sounds, but I promise I'm not here to cause you any harm. I made a promise to your husband that I would deliver a message to you, and now I've done just that. I'm sorry that I've upset you. That was not my intent, but I truly understand. My apologies for disturbing you."

He then turned away from the door and began walking down the porch steps to his car. Annie stood in the doorway and watched the young man walk slowly away. Her mind was awhirl with confusion. Who was he? Why did he show up out of nowhere, and how did he know anything about her husband? She continued to watch him as he reached the sidewalk, opened his car door, and got inside.

* * *

Traise sat down in the driver's seat of his car, closed the door, hung his head down, and let out a deep sigh. He wasn't sure how he felt right now. Maybe this had been a waste of time. Maybe he shouldn't have made the long trip here. He felt bad that he had upset the lady, but what was done was done.

As he reached for the key to start the ignition, there was a light tap on the driver's side window. He looked up to see Annie standing there, looking at him with a sullen but resolute look on her face. He pushed the button on the armrest, and the window slowly descended.

As Traise looked up at her, Annie bent over slightly toward him and said, "I think you owe me an explanation."

Traise knew that she deserved just that. Even if the story was incredible and she probably wouldn't believe him, the look on her face told him that he had unfinished business. He nodded slightly to her in affirmation. "Yes Ma'am, I owe you that," he said.

Annie stood back up, still looking at him with apprehension. "So where exactly did you come from?" she asked.

Traise sat back in the seat of the car and responded, "About five hours away, on the Eastern Shore of Virginia."

Annie, still with a sense of skepticism, crossed her arms and said, "You mean you drove all that way this morning to come here to tell somebody you never met before that you had a message from her dead husband?"

When she said it, it occurred to Traise just how unrealistic it sounded. "Believe it or not, Mrs. Hartman, that's exactly what I did."

Annie always felt that she was a good judge of character, and, as she looked into this young man's eyes, she experienced no sense of trepidation or concern for her safety. To her, his eyes had sincerity and honesty in them. She trusted her judgment and decided that she needed to hear what he had to say.

"You look like you could use a cup of coffee," Annie said at last. "So why don't you come in and tell me how you ended up here."

Chapter Seven

The warm wind of the summer air rushed around Bo Davidson as he pushed the accelerator down to pass a slower car on the two-lane road from his house in Buffalo Mills to Hyndman. With the beautiful weather, he had decided to take his '69 Mustang convertible for today's outing with Annie. She always liked the car and often kidded him about not driving it that much. It was a classic that he had spent many hours restoring from the old rusted heap that he had bought from an old farmer a few years back. The sun glistened off the immaculate, shiny red paint as he cruised effortlessly past the slow-poke and returned to the right lane of the road, the dual exhaust rumbling as he kept up speed down Route 96.

Bo was running a few minutes late because it had taken him longer than anticipated to take the cover off the car, put the top down, and give the entire vehicle a quick once over, cleaning any sign of dust or imperfection off the finish. The only time he ever took the "stang" out was in perfect weather. This was his baby, and he treated her as such. Since he was taking his favorite girl out for the afternoon, he figured it would be appropriate to take out his other favorite lady to match.

He slowed as he approached the sharp, almost ninety-degree left turn just outside town and only sped up slightly to forty miles an hour as he cruised past the old middle school, which was now a lumberyard, then the small town Little League field on the right. He had played many a game for the visiting Bedford team on that field back in the day when the uniforms were made of wool and almost as heavy as the young boys that wore them.

It only took about fifteen minutes to reach the main street of Hyndman, which, for some unknown reason, was not named "Main Street," but Center Street instead. He passed the bank on the right and slowed even more as he approached the yellow-flashing light at the intersection. Then he turned right onto Shellsburg Street and finally reached his destination at Annie's house on the left. He pulled the car to the side of the curb and turned off the ignition, taking a quick glance into the rearview mirror to check his appearance.

"Not bad. Not bad at all," he said hopefully as he turned the key, stopping the purr from the engine. He opened the door and spritely exited the vehicle, ready to pick up Annie and looking forward to a nice afternoon together. Hopping up the porch steps, he stopped, pulled open the screened door, gave a quick knock-knock, and cracked the door open slightly.

"Hey, anybody home?" he called out slightly louder than usual. Hearing nothing in return, he again knocked on the doorframe. "Annie? You here?" Again, he heard nothing from inside the house and instantly became concerned. This was not like her. She was always ready when they had plans. He slowly opened the door to the house and took a few steps inside. There was no indication of anyone inside, not even Hannah greeting him like she always did.

He moved slowly through the living room and into the kitchen. The screened door to the rear porch was open, and Bo saw Annie sitting in one of the chairs, staring out into the backyard, Hannah lying at her feet.

"Annie, you okay?" he said through the screen.

Startled, Annie jumped slightly at the sound of his voice and turned her head towards him. "Bo!" she said as soon as she saw him. "I'm sorry, I didn't hear you."

It was clear to Bo that something was wrong. Annie's body language and facial expression were unlike anything he had seen with her before. She looked exhausted and seemed to have something heavy on her mind. Then he noticed that she was clutching a framed photo on her lap.

He knew the picture because he had seen it many times before.

"Rough day with memories?" he asked as he stepped out onto the porch and took a seat beside her.

Annie looked down at the photo and gently rubbed her fingers over the picture. "To tell you the truth, I'm not sure," she said as she looked up and into his eyes.

He reached over and took one of her hands into his. "You want me to leave and give you some time to yourself?" Bo asked gently.

Annie shook her head slightly and squeezed his hand. "Not at all," she said. "I'm glad you're here, more than you know. Give me a few minutes and I'll be ready to go."

She released his hand, stood up from the chair, and put her hand gently on his shoulder as she walked in front of him and into the house.

Bo remained seated, not knowing what was going on or how to approach the rest of the day. This was not what he was expecting, and he was lost as to what to do or say. He hated seeing Annie in pain when her past came back to haunt her. He took a deep breath, saying to himself, "Well, this day just took a sudden turn."

True to her word, in just a few minutes, Annie reappeared at the screen door. "I'm ready if you're ready Bo."

Bo stood up from the chair and turned towards her. "You sure you're up for this? We can reschedule for another time."

Annie smiled slightly and responded, "I'm fine, and it'll be good to get out for a while. Besides, it's a beautiful day and I don't want to spend it here."

Annie looked down at Hannah, who was still lying on the porch floor fast asleep, "Come on, girl," she said to her little friend as she opened the screened door. Hannah opened her eyes and quickly got up to scamper into the kitchen.

Bo held the door as he followed the terrier inside. "Beautiful day indeed," he said. "I figure we'll head to the mall for a bit, maybe walk around downtown, and then grab a bite to eat if that works for you."

Annie reached out and squeezed his arm lightly. "That sounds great. Let's get going."

As they walked through the living room to the front door to leave, they both passed in front of the fireplace. Bo happened to notice that the picture Annie was holding earlier and was always on the mantel had been placed face down instead of its usual position beside the other photos. *That's strange,* he thought to himself as they continued out of the house.

Annie closed and locked the door and began making her way to the steps when Bo grabbed her hand and stopped her before she reached the first step. She turned slightly towards him, looking at him inquisitively. "Why don't we have a seat for a minute?" he said as he squeezed her hand and pointed to the swing at the end of the porch. Without a word, he guided her to the swing and sat down first, still holding onto her hand.

"I think we need to talk," he said. Annie sat down close beside him with her head lowered slightly. Bo continued, "I've never seen you like this, so I know something's going on. Did you have another dream?"

Still looking down, Annie took a deep breath and let out a sigh. "No, no dream this time. I almost wish there was."

Releasing her hand, Bo reached up and lightly stroked her hair, speaking softly. "So what *did* happen? You know I'm here for you and you can tell me anything."

Annie raised her head and stared into his eyes. "It's not fair that I've put you through this," she said as tears began to form in her eyes.

Bo put his arm around her and pulled her closer to him. "I wouldn't want to be anywhere else in the world," he said as he reached with his other hand and gently wiped a tear from her cheek. "Now, tell me what's going on."

* * *

Minutes turned to hours as Annie let go of over thirty years of emotions. Bo never released her hand as the pain, heartache, anger, confusion, and more poured from her soul. In all this time, she had never shared with anyone the feelings that she endured all to herself. She lost her husband so early and then her son to the sea without any solid explanation or closure. She lived with a constant hole in her heart that had never healed, always imagining what could have been and what she was robbed of ... growing old with the man she loved, watching their son grow together. The birthdays that weren't, family Thanksgiving dinners that never happened, the Christmases that should have been, the sound of grandchildren laughing and playing, sharing a walk in the fall as the leaves turned, seeing smiles or hearing Josh cuss when he screwed up something simple. All these experiences were taken from her, and she didn't know why.

The dreams she had were the only connection she still had that felt real. And she knew that even those were only alive in her mind. That is, until the visit earlier in the day from a stranger that had shaken her to her core. The unbelievable story that he told her and a message, albeit only two words, from Josh. That wasn't possible, was it? But what if it was? Could it really be that there is something else, somewhere that our loved ones exist? Are they really still with us, watching us as we continue on? Finding ways to let us know that they see us and wanting to somehow comfort us? She was more confused than ever. Her heart wanted to believe, but it just wasn't logical, was it?

Bo stayed silent the entire time Annie spoke. He let her cry when she needed to cry, let her shake when the anger and frustration overtook her, and he held her tightly with her head on his shoulder when the words ceased.

It took a few minutes for her to regain her composure. She wiped her eyes and pulled back from him slightly. "I'm so sorry, Bo. I've known how you feel about me, and I've felt the same for you. I just haven't been able to show it. All of this has made me hold back. I felt it just wasn't right for you to have this burden and craziness."

Bo pulled her back to him, looking at her face to face and into her eyes and noticed something different. Her gaze didn't seem so despondent anymore. Her inner struggle appeared to have eased. He held her face in his hands and as he gently caressed her cheeks with his thumbs said, "I'm here for you, any day, any night. Through thick and thin. I promise you will never have to go through anything alone again." He then kissed her on her forehead, looked again into her eyes, and said, "Ever."

Annie smiled as she pulled away slightly. "I'm a mess. What do you say I get straight and we go for a ride somewhere?"

Bo smiled back. "Sounds good to me," he said. "But I have to say that the story the young man told you sounds pretty out there."

Annie stood up from the swing, nodded her head, and said, "Stay right there. I want to show you something." She walked to the screen door, opened it, unlocked the front door, and went inside. In just a few seconds she reemerged and sat down again beside Bo. She held out a small piece of paper to him.

"What's this?" Bo asked as he took the paper from her.

"Just read it," she said as he began to unfold it. On the paper were only a few words on two lines. The first line read, "Annie Hartman, Hyndman, Pa." The second line had her address written but in handwriting different from the first. Bo looked at the paper and the words then up to Annie.

"I don't understand," he said.

Annie looked along with Bo as they both examined the small note. "The second line was written by the young man who visited me this morning."

129

Bo continued looking at the note and said, "Well, who wrote the first line?"

They both raised their heads and looked at each other as Annie said, "The first line is Josh's handwriting, I compared it to the letters that he wrote me when he was on the ship before he disappeared."

Bo's eyebrows went up, his eyes widened, and his jaw dropped. He looked back at the note as Annie stood up and walked toward the door. "Give me a minute and we'll head out," she said as she disappeared inside.

* * *

The moon was just peeking over the mountains surrounding Hyndman, Pennsylvania, on the summer's early evening as Bo and Annie climbed into the glimmering red Mustang convertible.

"Top up or top down?" Bo asked as he turned the ignition and the engine came to life.

"It's still warm, so I say top down," Annie said as she reached for the seat belt.

Bo nodded once. "Top down it is. So where to, ma'am?"

Annie reached over and placed her hand on top of Bo's as he held the gear shift, ready to put the car into drive. She looked up into the clear, darkening sky at the fully lit moon now in full view over the mountains. "Let's just follow the moon and see where it takes us."

She then leaned over toward him and motioned with a single finger. Following her lead, he leaned in as well. They came together and their lips touched for the first time. As she pulled back slightly, Annie smiled and looked deeply into the eyes of the man that loved her and who, she now knew, she could love back.

"Follow the moon indeed," Bo said as he smiled, put the car into drive, and they pulled away.

High above and unnoticed by the two as they drove into the country, a solitary entity streaked across the sky, its glimmering and sparkling tail trailing behind. As the single point of light passed before the glowing moon, its brightness increased suddenly to an almost explosive apex, then faded quickly.

* * *

The dream began just as it had so many times before, with Annie sitting in a small wooden boat drifting through the fog towards the dock. She could see the outline of a lone figure standing at the end of the structure as the mist began to lift. She could now see Josh, just as she remembered him: young, handsome, and vibrant. Two other figures were now also visible behind him although she couldn't see them clearly. One appeared to be an older man wearing shorts and a ragged shirt, and the other appeared to be about the same age as Josh.

As the boat closed in on the dock, Josh held up his right arm, gave a slow wave to her, and mouthed the words, "It's okay."

The older man came up beside him and put his arm around Josh's shoulder and waved as well. The third figure, Annie now recognized as her son J.J. He stood beside the other two and raised his hand and waved to his mother. She was now close enough to see him clearly as he smiled and formed the words, "I love you Mom" to her.

As Annie drew the warmth of those words into her heart, the boat began to drift backward away from the dock. The fog thickened as she strained to see the three on the dock. Just before she lost sight of them, all three gave a final wave, turned, and began to disappear into the mist up the dock until they were no more.

* * *

Annie's eyes slowly opened as the morning sunshine broke through her window. She turned her head and saw Hannah curled up on the bed beside her and gave the terrier a rub on the head. "Good morning girl," she said, and then she lifted her arms above her head, stretched, and pulled herself up to a sitting position. She was slightly startled at the sound of movement in the kitchen and looked at the closed bedroom door as it slowly opened.

"One cream and two sugars?" Bo said as he stood in the opened doorway with two cups. "Looks like it's going to be a great day," he said as he handed her one of the cups.

Annie looked up at Bo as she accepted the steaming cup of coffee, smiled, and took a sip. "Yes it is," she said. "The first of many."

About the Author

Herm Rawlings grew up in Hyndman, Pennsylvania, graduating from high school in 1979. He enlisted in the United States Coast Guard the same year. He retired in 1999 at the rank of Chief Petty Officer, Hospital Corpsman. He married his wife Kim in 1984 while stationed at Group Eastern Shore in Chincoteague, Virginia. He and Kim have one son, Traise, who was born in 1987 while they were stationed at the Coast Guard Air Station in Sacramento, California. During his career, he and his family lived in multiple locations, such as Cape Hatteras, North Carolina; Yorktown, Virginia; Governors Island, New York; and Norfolk, Virginia. He also served aboard two Coast Guard Cutters, the Cherokee, ported in Little Creek, Virginia, and the Tamaroa, ported in Portsmouth, New Hampshire.

Following his retirement from the Coast Guard after twenty years, Herm and his family returned to the Chincoteague area on the Eastern Shore of Virginia. He re-entered government service in 2001 when he accepted his current position as the Navy Installation Housing Director for the Surface Combat Systems Center, located at Wallops Island, Virginia.

In the mid-2000s, Herm became "The Good Doctor," as the host of a popular afternoon radio show on WCTG in Chincoteague. After five years on the radio, Herm was half of the *Herm and Rayce Show*, the first internet-based live audio/video stream show on the Eastern Shore. He also created an internet solo project, *TerraRadioOnline*, that ran for two years.

Herm has always enjoyed writing and has had multiple pieces published in local periodicals, including as an active contributor to *Shore Secrets Magazine*.

Herm's first book, the well-received *Family Tradition*, was published by Scantic Books in 2019. *Family Tradition* tells the gripping tale of Joshua Hartman as a young Coast Guard sailor and how he came to join his grandfather after being lost at sea while on patrol.

Made in the USA
Middletown, DE
29 October 2023